I0733240

Poppy

CHRIS KENISTON

Indie House Publishing

This book is a work of fiction. Names, characters, places, and incidents are the product of the author's imagination or are used fictionally. Any resemblance to actual events, locales, or persons, living or dead, is coincidental.

Copyright © 2020 Christine Baena

All rights reserved. No part of this book may be reproduced, scanned, redistributed or transmitted in any form or by any means, print, electronic, mechanical, photocopying, recording, or otherwise, without prior written permission of Author.

Indie House Publishing

BOOKS BY CHRIS KENISTON

Hart Land
Heather
Lily
Violet
Iris
Hyacinth
Rose
Calytrix
Zinnia
Poppy

Farraday Country
Adam
Brooks
Connor
Declan
Ethan
Finn
Grace
Hannah
Ian
Jamison
Keeping Eileen
Loving Chloe
Morgan

Aloha Series Heartwarming Edition
Aloha Texas
Almost Paradise
Mai Tai Marriage
Dive Into You

Look of Love
Love by Design
Love Walks In
Flirting with Paradise

Surf's Up Flirts
(Aloha Series Companions)
Shall We Dance
Love on Tap
Head Over Heels
Perfect Match
Just One Kiss
It Had to Be You

**Other Books
By Chris Keniston**

Honeymoon Series
Honeymoon for One
Honeymoon for Three
Honeymoon for Four

Family Secrets Novels
Champagne Sisterhood
The Homecoming
Hope's Corner

Original Aloha Series
Waikiki Wedding

ACKNOWLEDGEMENTS

What a fun journey this has been through Hart Land and the lives of all the fun characters. As I write the last of the nine granddaughters, I am amazed how quickly time has gone by.

This has been a challenging year for many people, and I hope that Hart Land has offered at least a little escape from the chaos.

In order to bring this last story to you, I truly relied on a good many help for inspiration and brainstorming. Olivia Rigal, I can't imagine the book without the brownies. Kathy Ivan, I would never get anything done without your constant support. Dale Mayer, you are the epitome of good sport and a great plot solving mind! Laura Scott, it was ever so nice getting to pick your plotting brain.

And of course, we could not have another Hart Land book without a family recipe, and for this I must thank our cousin Patty Healy for her grandmother's depression cake recipe! You're the best!

Enjoy and look forward to gathering together again with the next series!

PROLOGUE

"**I** don't see any way around this. Dylan isn't easy."

"I beg your pardon?" General Richard Powell, U.S. Marine Corps Retired, spoke up via Zoom from the tablet perched on the credenza. "What's wrong with my grandson?"

"Face it. He's not in local real estate, he doesn't fish, he's not in charge of an annual picnic, and he doesn't need a place to stow away to write the great American novel. We've been at this for hours. There's simply no way to bring these two together."

"It doesn't help any that his work isn't exactly portable." Cole's granddad, Captain Donald McIntyre USN Retired, shrugged.

"We just need to think harder." Harold knew his Poppy and Dick's grandson Dylan would be perfect for each other. They just needed to come up with a casual way to *accidentally* get them in the same place at the same time.

"Why is this match so difficult? We're eight for eight and it never took this long to come up with an idea." Jake's grandfather, Commander Eugene Harper USN Retired, heaved a deep sigh.

Flipping his palm face up, Don made a who-the-hell-knows gesture. "Maybe it's the church."

"What does the church have to do with anything?" Gene lifted his gaze from the cards in his hand.

"Something about playing cards in the pastor's counseling office doesn't feel right."

"Too risky getting together at Hart House and having someone overhear or put eight and eight together. Besides, it's not like we're playing poker or betting."

Don shrugged. "You're right. We're not plotting to rob the Pope or anything nefarious. Just giving two people well suited to each other a little nudge toward happily ever after. That's sort of the Lord's work."

"It is a nice church." Frank's gaze danced around them at the dark wood paneling, the intricately carved trim work surrounding the built-in bookcases, and the exquisite murals on the ceiling and walls reminiscent of the great churches of Europe. "What is it, a hundred years old?"

"Almost two hundred." The old fieldstone-based building with cedar shingles and a wooden steeple tower that could be seen almost to the next county had been the heart of Lawford Mountain for generations. "The stained glass windows are newer. About a hundred and twenty years or so. When we leave I'll take you into the sanctuary. The handcrafted features and hand-painted murals will leave you in awe. The sad thing is that anything this old needs lots of reworking. The plumbing is constantly leaking and the tree roots are in constant battle with the sewer lines. When I offered the pastor a little donation to use the church on his day off for my men's club meeting, he was quick to accept."

"I'll chip in some," one of the voices added, followed by another and another.

Frank nodded. "I'm in too. Now, back to the final match. You said Poppy works here long hours?"

"Some days, yes. Depends on what the church board is up to and how much backup the pastor needs." Harold reached into his pocket and handed out four Cuban cigars, one for each of his buddies and one for himself. "Maybe this will help inspire us. Since there's no bourbon here, next best thing is a good smoke."

"Where did you get these?"

Harold bit back a smile. "I still have a few connections."

"You're not supposed to be smoking those," Dick's voice boomed from the nearby tablet.

"It's been over a year since this damn rollercoaster ride started. I'm doing great. Fit as a fiddle. Monthly treatments are over. I've been promoted to every six months for follow up." Harold wouldn't admit—even to his lifelong buddies—that he'd been scared to death when diagnosed, and had been lucky as hell that all he'd needed to fight this miserable disease was outpatient surgery and monthly immunotherapy.

"That does sound good." Don focused on his playing cards. "I'll bid two."

"It is. At this point one cigar won't hurt. The best war games were planned with a stiff drink whenever possible, but always with a cigar." As challenging as the diagnosis over a year ago had been, at least it had spurred him on when it came to his granddaughters. He'd waited long enough for them to make their own matches. It was time.

"Hal's right. All it took was a few turns of the wrench and when that faucet fell off, my Jake was practically on his way down the aisle." Gene set his cigar in the make-shift ashtray. "Pass."

"And despite the tragedy of Adele, we managed to get Eric and the kids to Hart Land."

"In the nick of time too." Retired Marine Corps Colonel Francis—Frank—Peterson peered over the cards in his hands.

"Why didn't Gil fly in?" Don asked about Iris' grandfather-in-law, Captain Gilbert Johnson USN Retired.

"Fishing with his son." Frank smiled at his cards. "Four."

"You know I can't pass up a four bid." Harold reached for the kitty of cards in the middle of the table.

"I know." Frank grinned. "Some things haven't changed one iota since Annapolis. I almost said five."

Ignoring Dick's contented smirk, Harold slid the four new cards into his hand. He and his academy cohorts had three more days together before Gene and Frank had to fly home. Something would come to mind. It had to. Making multiple grandfathers visiting at the same time look like a coincidence hadn't been easy. Of course, there was always Fate. She did a pretty good job at improvisation. Lily hitting Cole with her car had been sheer genius on her part. Not that he wished Dylan to be hit by a car, but Harold was confident between the four of them here in this room and the rest of their matchmaking troops available when needed, thanks to the modern cyber world, a plan would be hatched sooner or later.

Don took a puff of his cigar and moved the ashtray out of the way and onto the small cabinet under the nearby window. "We could wait for winter and pray for an avalanche."

"An avalanche?" Harold stopped sorting his cards.

"Yeah, you know, like that movie where the men and women were all snowbound in a small cabin for the winter. Spent most of the time dancing."

"*Seven Brides for Seven Brothers*?" Frank frowned.

"Maybe." Don shrugged.

"We're not waiting till winter, and we're not burying anyone under an avalanche of snow." Harold set four cards aside. Crazy stunts like that were his housekeeper Lucy's type of shenanigans, and even *she* wouldn't go that far. "Clubs are trump."

Frank sniffed at the air. "How old is the wiring in this place?"

"Old enough. Why?" A familiar and unpleasant smell tickled at Harold's nose.

The other card players paused and sniffed.

"Something's burning." Don pushed to his feet and his eyes grew wide as he reached for the cigar that was no longer on the cabinet.

Arm straight out, Gene pointing at the large window behind them just as a burst of flames exploded from the trash can. "Where's the fire extinguisher?"

"In the hall!" someone shouted.

The flames licked at the edge of the old velvet drapes. Don kicked the wastebasket away as the other men lurched toward the window, too late to prevent the drapes from going up in flames.

"Oh, hell." Now Frank was stomping on the burning papers scattered across the throw rug atop two hundred year old pine floors.

Gene hurried back into the small room. "Oh, sh—"

Beating at the fiery rug with the shirts off their backs and the flames spreading to piles of papers despite their efforts, and the extinguisher, Harold stopped and whipped out his phone. No sense going through dispatch, Cole was on speed dial. "The church is on fire."

By the time the sound of sirens had the men rushing outdoors, the pastor had come from his house across the street and turned on the garden hose. Don commandeered the neighbor's hose and watered down the cedar shingles. Harold gave a silent prayer of thanks that the place wasn't totally engulfed in tongues of fire. The Lord had one heck of a way of reminding him smoking cigars was not good for his health. Or anyone else's. Especially a two hundred year old wooden building. Fiona was going to kill him.

"I don't know how the ashtray tipped over." His face painted with guilt, Don stood at his side.

"That was my fault." Gene sighed. "I bumped the cabinet with my foot. Probably knocked it over."

"I was sitting right there." Lips pressed tightly together, Don shook his head. "I should have heard the thing fall into the basket. Should have moved the basket."

"It could have been me," Harold said. "My ashtray was on the other end. Maybe I nudged it. What matters is we did our best to contain it."

The fire trucks pulled up, and like ants escaping a knocked over hill, scurrying to protect their larvae, firemen ran in every direction. Hoses spewed water at the historical building. The sound of smashed glass filled the air and Harold bit down hard on his back teeth, praying the noise wasn't one of the ancient stained glass windows or the treasured artwork.

"That couldn't be good."

"Or could it?" Frank tipped his head and turned to his friends, smiling.

For a moment Harold thought senility had taken over Frank's thoughts. Then he got it. A slow grin tugged at his cheeks. "I'll be. Fate—and the firemen—did it again."

CHAPTER ONE

"I feel like a soggy rat after a flash flood." Poppy stood at her desk. The Lawford Mountain Community Church had survived almost two hundred years of winter, rain, drought, feast and famine. She wasn't so sure it was going to survive one cigar.

"It's not that bad." Pastor Robert Sullivan, her boss for the most part and known to all as Bob, smiled at her as if all the pieces of paper on or in her desk hadn't inflated like a sponge to three times its size.

Well, not in width and length, but the few sheets that had dried since the firemen turned off the torrent of water were stacked much higher, and many no longer fit in folders.

"The water restoration people should be here any minute," the pastor reminded her. They'd been called as soon as the firemen left the scene and informed him and the church board that the building hadn't sustained enough structural damage to preclude any efforts at rescue.

Her gaze traveled from one corner of the room to the other and out the doorway. Even in the brief amount of time it had taken the local fire department to put out the rapidly spreading fire, it had been more than enough time to soak the few rugs the church offices had. Scurrying to salvage as much as possible, she'd sloshed through the water along with half the town. People had come with their own push brooms and floor mops in an effort to drain the pooling water away from the old pine floors. The sorry scene almost made her want to cry. The church was already struggling to keep up with this beautiful, but old, edifice. They really didn't need fire and flood on top of everyday wear and tear.

Hands on her hips, Lucy nodded. "I agree with the pastor. We did a darned good job."

"You'll earn extra rewards in heaven for this." Grams stood on tippy toe and kissed Zinnia's fiancé, David's, cheek. "If we had to wait for the flood restoration people to get here before removing all this water, these floors would have been ruined."

"And the walls," Jake, the most recent grandson-in-law added to the clan, said. "Sheetrock soaks up water faster than a thirsty man fresh out of the desert."

The turnout from town to help had been heartwarming. Jake had brought over every floor squeegee and wet vacuum he had in stock at the hardware store. Mabel from the diner had contributed a nonstop supply of hot coffee and tea. Poppy's sister Lily had kept all the volunteers energized with both sugary and protein-heavy treats from the Pastry Stop. Katie from the One Stop kept everyone hydrated with bottles of water and sports drinks.

At one point, with so many bodies bumping into each other trying to sweep the water out the door, vacuum up the water, or carry out whatever treasured pieces of furniture and artwork weren't bolted down, the pastor finally had to send some people home and ask them to please just pray. Poppy wanted to also suggest they give a little extra in next week's collection box, but decided if ever there was a time to keep her mouth closed, this would be one of them. People had given so much already.

Glancing out the window, the front yard of the church looked like a sorry attempt at a tag sale. The Merry Widows and most of her cousins were toweling down the wooden furniture they'd successfully removed before it soaked up anymore of the water. Some neighbors held blow dryers plugged into orange extension cords and aimed at the furniture to help with the deep-down drying. Metal cabinets and wastebaskets were scattered about. At least odds were in their favor that the sun would continue to shine until it was safe to move all the belongings back inside.

"You look awfully pensive." Her grandmother slipped an arm around her waist. "It will be fine. You'll see."

"I know." Somewhere deep in her heart Poppy knew everything would work out, but the images in the back of her mind stuttered her heart every step of the way. Obviously the curtains were gone and would have to be replaced along with the scorched walls, and probably smoke stained ceiling. But it was the gorgeous artwork that normally hung in the counseling room that left her so doubtful. How would they undo the smoke and water damage? With all their other woes, she wasn't sure the church carried enough insurance for the cost of such a major undertaking.

"You're still frowning." Grams wiped at her forehead with her thumb. "Have I ever lied to you?"

That brought a smile to Poppy's face. "No, ma'am."

"There you go." Grams retreated a step, her linked fingers lingering slightly until she fully let go. "Now let's see if we can find out how long thoroughly drying this place out is going to take, or if we need to set an office up for you and Pastor Bob at Hart House."

Wiggling her toes within her damp shoes, Poppy looked down at her soiled and slightly torn skirt. The thing had seen better days. Maybe camping out at Hart House for work would be the silver lining on today's fire. Actually, an angel from heaven appearing out of thin air and putting the place back together the way it was—murals, craftsmanship, and all—would be perfect. After all, she really *did* believe in miracles.

• • • •

"Oh, that does look beautiful." General Richard—Dick—Powell smiled at his grandson. "Your grandmother is going to love this."

"I certainly hope so." Dylan had to agree with his grandfather that the odds were pretty good his grandmother would indeed love the painting. The project was definitely turning out better than he'd expected. It had been years since he'd attempted anything original for his own pleasure. The hope was that this portrait of his sister's children and his grandmother would be the perfect gift for her upcoming birthday.

From the other room he could hear his business line ring and the phone's answering machine pick up. Screening calls was a necessity when he was deep in a project. "This is Pastor Bob Sullivan from Lawford Mountain in New England. We've had a recent… *incident* at our church and would like to get an idea of your fees and availability." The man hesitated a long beat before adding, simply, "Thank you."

His grandfather's gaze darted back and forth to the hall doorway and back to Dylan, almost intentionally averting the phone as if it might reach out and bite him. What was that all about?

The business line rang again.

Having kept his focus on the painting in front of him, he'd barely paid attention to the previous caller. A second call within minutes had his head snapping up.

"This is General Harold Hart. I've been told on good authority that you're the best in the business. You should be hearing soon from Pastor Robert Sullivan. The church will of course be having a bazaar or some other event to raise funds for your services, as well as your travel expenses from Texas." The voice cleared his throat. "I would like to make a major—anonymous—contribution to the fund. Please get in touch with me as soon as possible." The rough voice that sounded every bit a Marine disconnected the call. Though for all Dylan knew, army generals sounded as rough and gruff as Marine Corps generals. Maybe even the air force. But a general *and* a pastor? An interesting combination off the battle field. "Odd."

"What is?" His granddad frowned at the canvas in front of Dylan.

"Not the painting. The two phone calls."

"What's so odd about two phone calls?" On that question the phone rang one more time.

Once again, the voicemail system kicked in. "Hello Mr. Powell, this is Nadine Baker. Your name has been floated around as someone who can be trusted with a two hundred year old building."

Poised for the next stroke, the hand holding the paint brush lowered slowly to the palette of pastel colors. The words *two hundred year old* had caught his attention.

"The town will of course be responsible for your fee, but the Merry Wid—my women's group—would like to contribute anonymously to the cause."

Today seemed to be the day for charitable hearts.

"If you could kindly return my call to discuss figures before you speak with Pastor Sullivan that would be very nice. Thank you."

"*That's* what's odd about *three* phone calls." Now he put the palette down on the nearby table, swirled his brush in the jar, and let his mind turn with curiosity.

"This can't be the first time you've had three phone calls in a day."

"Perhaps not in a day, but certainly back to back and all about a pastor."

"You mean a church." Lowering his chin to peer at his grandson over the brim of his eyeglasses, the retired general's voice dropped a few notches as well. "I know you've done church restorations before."

He had. It was some of his favorite work, depending on the need. The two projects in Italy had been his most enjoyable. "Yes."

"So what makes these calls so odd?"

"Usually I deal with one person and any anonymous donations would be made to the church, not to me."

"Oh, well. I wouldn't know about that." His grandfather took a step back and a deep breath. "Are you interested?"

Keeping quiet, Dylan proceeded to clean his brushes. He'd pick up again tomorrow in better light and with a clear head. "Maybe." Truth was, he was more than interested. How many chances did a man have to work in the United States on two hundred year old artwork? But it was his grandfather's curiosity that had his interest at the moment. "So, what aren't you telling me?"

As expected, his grandfather snapped around. Eyes wide with surprise—or guilt—blinked, dropping the military veil of authority to hide whatever was going on in that complex mind of his. "What makes you ask that?"

"Just a hunch." Something about the way his grandfather looked lost somewhere between awkward and uncomfortable made him think perhaps the old man knew more than he was letting on. Though what the connection could be between his grandfather and an ancient small-town church was beyond him. Maybe he'd been watching too many reruns of *Law and Order*. He was developing a cynical mind.

His granddad hesitated, seeming to search for his words. Another oddity in its own right. The former Marine Corps general was never at a loss for words. "There isn't much to tell. Recently a friend mentioned there's been a fire at his local church. A very old building with murals. Stories got kicked around about restoring the Mona Lisa and the Sistine Chapel and somewhere in there your name and the recent job you did for the Atlanta Museum of Art came up."

"The Mona Lisa has never been fully restored. Too risky."

"Yes, that was mentioned. Anyhow, these calls may or may not have something to do with that recent conversation. After all, you are one of the best in the country. Why shouldn't they want you?"

Well, there was nothing nefarious in his grandfather discussing art or bringing up that Dylan was indeed a conservator/restorer of fine art by trade. And his reputation had indeed grown to national recognition in recent years. So why did he have this strange nagging feeling, reminiscent of a small spider loose and crawling up his back?

CHAPTER TWO

"I can't believe how much they've gotten done in such a short amount of time." Poppy sorted the last pile of papers on the filing cabinet.

Gently running his fingers across the aged oak desk, Pastor Bob smiled up at her. "The goodness in people's hearts and the kindness of strangers never ceases to amaze me."

There was no way Poppy was going to spit back that he sounded like a paraphrased line from the old movie, *A Streetcar Named Desire*. Definitely inappropriate for church conversation. Though at the moment the church truly was relying on the kindness of strangers. Strangers from all over the mountain, bordering states, and even a few experts from out of state had made appearances to donate, assist, or put in a few good hours of hard labor. Either way, it was all a labor of love. Too bad the insurance company wasn't feeling as generous. A lot had been done but sometimes it felt like with every item checked off the to-do list, another problem was uncovered. And hardly ever a simple problem. Sourcing matching two hundred year old oak plank flooring was neither easy nor inexpensive.

"Another day and the window guys will be out from underfoot." The pastor checked off another task in his day planner. The man wasn't much older than Poppy but he liked keeping track of his world the old-fashioned way—with paper and pen. Perhaps that made the growing list seem less daunting. "Looks like the church yard sale is coming together just in the nick of time."

Most of the repairs so far had been smaller projects done with donated supplies and labor and lots of well meaning volunteer work sprinkled in. Bills were piling up, and the bigger projects were yet to be tackled. Brent, the best contractor in Lawford, had donated plenty of time to carefully remove the old wainscoting and soggy plaster until the insurance settled, but the man had bills to pay too. Then there was the art restoration. The congregation had quickly organized a tag sale to raise immediate funds so work wouldn't have to stop, but still.

"Here's a list of the donations from the shops on Main Street." Pastor Bob stretched out his hand. "As soon as you're done there, would you mind running into town to pick them up? Since your grandmother is in charge of the donations, you might as well just call it an early day and stay home when you deliver the collection."

"Perfect timing." She slammed the last cabinet drawer closed. "We now have all our alphabetized records at our fingertips once again." She loved a neat and orderly office, even if there were more exposed two by fours than actual walls. The chaos of the last couple of weeks was driving her mad, although she did love watching the church slowly come back to life. Most of the woodwork had never looked so bright and clean. She hadn't realized how much darker years of daily dirt and grime had made the place. And it certainly hadn't occurred to her that removing the layers of smoke and soot would take with it all those years of dirt and leave behind a rich, glowing, and more colorful wood. Once the whole building was finished the results were going to be a much brighter workplace. That was, as long as they could come up with the money. And they would, she decided. Everyone was doing their best. Things had to come together.

"Oh," Pastor scribbled one more name on the bottom, "Edna from Buy the Book has a few gifts to use on a bid system."

Poppy nodded. "That should be good. She always comes across such interesting old editions."

"That she does," he agreed.

Slinging her purse over her shoulder, Poppy reached for her hat and dropped it on her head. "I'll be on my way and will see you tomorrow."

"Sounds good." The pastor waved, that single barely moving motion like the Queen, and returned his attention to the papers on his desk.

Poppy organized the donors so that she could park her car and walk down one side of Main Street and then back up the other. Slamming her car door, she turned and flattened her hat on her head with one hand. She probably shouldn't have worn such a wide brim on a breezy day, but she'd been in a whimsical mood when she'd dressed this morning and her favorite hat reminded her of spring, making it the perfect final touch.

First stop on the list: Betty at the Cut and Set. As long as Betty wasn't donating one of those old-school stand-up hairdryers that looked like an alien from outer space, she should be able to fit all the donations in the box she'd grabbed from the storage room. Two coupons for a mani-pedi secured, she continued on to Floyd's to collect a hand-carved chess set.

"Thank you, Floyd. It's lovely." And it really was. The pieces stored easily in a well-lined case that unhinged to form the chess table. Small pieces of what looked like mother of pearl were inlaid in a design around the border of the squares. "Just beautiful. Are you sure you want to part with it?"

Floyd nodded. "It's for a very good cause."

A few more words of appreciation and she moved along. Batting back and forth whether or not it would be ethical if she bid on the set herself, she reached Edna's. The small bookshop had been a favorite haunt of hers as a teen. As much as Poppy enjoyed a quiet paperback by the lake from time to time, there was something almost magical about reading a novel in the big old easy chair in the corner, surrounded by wall after wall of shelved books. That was probably one of the reasons she loved working at the church. Her office had once been the pastor's library and the wooden cases across from her desk were once again stocked heavily with books that, by the grace of God, weren't totally drowned in water, merely sprinkled. Lightly. Edna had assured her that most of the dampened tomes could be saved and so far she was right.

"Oh good." Edna hurried out from behind a counter waving a small, leather-bound book. Poppy knew it had to be a big deal whenever she saw Edna handling a book with white gloves. "This should fetch a goodly amount."

Every so often someone would donate an item of above average value for one of the church yard sales and rather then put a price that no bargain hunter would pay, they would leave out a bid sheet, much like a silent auction, and if they got enough for it at the end of the day, the highest offer would win the donation. Poppy glanced down at the cover. *The Scarlet Letter*. She almost laughed. Earlier in the day, *A*

Street Car Named Desire's classic line uttered by Blanche Dubois came to mind, and now this classic on moral values of its day made an appearance. Bound in dark red leather with gold lettering and gilded pages, the book seemed in awfully good shape.

"This is a limited edition from 1971. I considered donating the second edition I have, but that would fetch a much better price in a real auction. So, here you go."

The woman handed off the book and Poppy looked down at her hands.

"Oh, you don't need gloves." Edna chuckled. "I was handling the second edition from 1850 just as you came in."

With a relieved nod, Poppy accepted the hardback. Adding a thank you and a smile, she proceeded to her next stop. By the time she'd made her rounds and arrived at KaBloom, the box was becoming rather cumbersome and the wind was picking up annoyingly. Standing in front of the flower shop, she decided it was time to cross the street and drop the box in her car before the next collection. The odds of the donation being one item too many were weighing heavily in her arms. Carefully glancing in each direction, she darted across the street, then balanced the box on one hip while using her free hand to battle the key fob.

Another gust of wind whipped past her and slapping her hand on her head to secure the hat, she almost dropped her keys. Box securely stashed in her car, she locked the door, took one step to cross the street, and the next breeze snatched her hat and sent it flying over her head. "Oh, no!"

Hat high above her, she reached out and the darn thing dipped out of her reach only to be lifted skyward again. "Blast!" Pushing off one foot like a cat about to pounce, she shot forward, chasing after the hat. Another gust, another dart and she felt like a kid chasing a kite tail controlled by someone else. *This was absurd.* This hat had more flight than a sparrow in spring. One more dash in its direction, her arm snapping after the flimsy chapeau, her foot came forward and unexpectedly collided with something hard. Glancing down, she had a moment to see a big dark shoe before the second big foot came stomping down. Smack on her favorite hat.

• • • •

What the… Dylan stepped out of the old-fashioned barber shop and ran smack dab into… something. Actually—some*one*. A very pretty, but clearly distressed, someone. "Excuse me." He offered a shaky smile and took two steps back.

A rushing gush of wind blew the door out of his hand and something underfoot lifted away. Big brown eyes widened on an already fretful face. "My hat!"

Her what? Dylan looked up, his gaze following the flying object and direction the lovely vision was now sprinting in. She was indeed chasing after what looked to be a wide brimmed straw hat. Who in their right mind wore a hat on a day like today?

Just as she reached the wind-carried cover, another draft blew the headgear away. The dots in his mind finally connecting, he hurried after the pretty brunette, nearly colliding with her when she stopped short and leaned over.

He could feel another burst of wind coming and before the hat in question took another flight down Main Street, he stretched his leg out, and more careful this time to merely trap an edge of the wide brim and not smash it, his foot landed with a thump.

Back snapped straight, her eyes bore into him. Not eyes filled with gratitude or appreciation as he lifted the hat from underfoot, but angry eyes.

"Here you go."

If she'd been a character in a children's storybook, now would have been the time that fire would flare from her nostrils. Instead, she sucked in a long deep breath that made her chest rise in the pastel blouse, then very slowly blew it out. Through clenched teeth she managed to mutter, "Thank you." The softly spoken words totally belying her tense countenance.

Long delicate fingers gripped the opposite side of the somewhat crumpled brim. Okay, maybe a bit more than somewhat, and maybe a bit more than crumpled. He had a large foot and even in the warm weather he'd worn his steel tipped boots. Perhaps stepping on the thing hadn't been his best idea, and unlike an old masterpiece, he knew nothing about hats but had enough common sense to determine this one might have seen the last of its days. "Sorry about that."

Fire flared behind those big brown eyes but once again her words came out soft, low, almost sweet. "It's fine. It's just a… hat."

The fire dimmed to a mournful stare and he knew enough to recognize when fine was anything but. "Maybe all it needs is a little reshaping." He stretched his hand forward, reaching for the crumpled edge and before his fingers made contact, she snapped it back against her chest.

"Really. It's fine. Thank you." Without another word, she spun on her heel and darted across the street.

It took all the self discipline he could muster to not run after her. If growing up with sisters had taught him anything, tangling with a newly upset female would be about as productive as wrestling an alligator with a thorn in its underbelly.

"Something wrong?" The General stepped out of the barbershop, nudging Dylan out of the way.

Turning his back to the distressed brunette, he shook his head. "No sir." At least he hoped not. "Just bumped into someone."

The old man's brows rose high on his forehead. "Oh."

"Yes, sir. No casualties." He smiled. Except the hat.

The General's gaze bounced from one end of the street to the other.

The pretty brunette must have darted into a store. Or perhaps driven off. She was nowhere in sight.

"You sure you don't want a rematch?" the General asked, a smile returning to his face.

Dylan shook his head. The crowd gathered inside for *friendly* games of checkers had the cutthroat instincts of a warrior tribe. They played to win. He preferred to settle into his cabin, take in the relaxing views, and get a good night's rest before meeting the pastor first thing in the morning.

"Shall we expect you for dinner this evening?"

"Thank you, but the only problem with an early morning flight is the need to get out of bed earlier than a Marine recruit."

The General actually held back a laugh. "You have your grandfather's sense of humor."

"Thank you, sir." Any comparison to his grandfather was always a good thing. "I'm going to unpack, have a light snack, and hit the sack early." But first he had an errand to run and then a little reconnaissance work to do. Somewhere there had to be a hatless brunette he owed an apology to.

CHAPTER THREE

"If yesterday's collection is any sign, this year's yard sale is going to be the best ever." With so much of the church undergoing renovations, and Grams in charge of donations, Poppy had volunteered to store the collected goods at Hart House. With Gram's permission, of course.

Lucy wiped her hand dry on the dishrag. "You joining us for breakfast? I was just about to pull the croissants out of the oven."

"Can't." Somehow last night she'd missed that a few items, including Floyd's chess set, had fallen out of the box and onto the car floor. "Just dropping these off before I head to the church. But," she grinned, "I might as well steal a warm croissant for the road."

"Warm croissants to go, coming right up. I'll toss in a couple more for Pastor and Brent." Lucy winked. "And I'm not the least bit surprised donations are up. Everybody wants to help this year."

"Now Lucy," Fiona Hart, matriarch of the clan, fingered the handmade chess set Poppy had set on the kitchen table, "the town wants to help every year. This year we simply have good reason to dig a little deeper."

The back door swung open, the sound of yipping and woofing drawing everyone's attention away from the scattered donations and over to a ball of fluff in each of Cindy's arms. Her gaze danced across the boxes of donations still stacked against the wall. "Who robbed a bank?"

Hyacinth's husband Alan followed his wife into the kitchen. Kicking the door shut with his foot, he placed two more squirming puppies on the ground. Within seconds, four furballs were scurrying around the kitchen island, chasing each other, skidding under the stools, slipping across the floors, and generally looking absolutely adorable. Well, all but one whose adorable was rather different from the rest of the litter.

"What have we here?" Grams leaned down to pick up the one

pup that was attacking the hem of her pants. "You're a feisty one, aren't you?"

"Reminds me of Sarge at that age." Moving closer to where Grams stood, Lucy scratched the blond little guy under his chin.

"Where did these cuties come from?" An almost white puppy ran circles around Poppy's ankles.

"Mrs. Nashua over in Belvedere took a tumble last night."

"Oh, no." Gram's looked up from the second puppy that had decided her other pant leg looked equally interesting.

"Broken hip. She's going to be laid up for a while. Since she lives alone, from the hospital she goes straight to rehab. There's no one to take care of these guys."

"Surely you have enough connections to find them homes?" Lucy asked.

"These are the last four. I already found homes for the first five."

"Nine puppies?" Poppy set the fussy one down on the ground. She really had to get moving.

"Mama is an English Cream Golden Retriever. Mrs. Nashua isn't sure who papa was. A rather unfortunate accident, otherwise they'd all be spoken for and at a high price." Cindy reached for a croissant. "We'll be fostering mama until Mrs. Nashua comes home. Betty said I could drop one pup off at the Cut and Set for the day, as did Jake at the hardware store, and Floyd at the barbershop in hopes someone will fall in love and take the puppy home."

"That's three. What are you going to do with the fourth?"

"Well," Cindy smiled sweetly at her grandmother, "this one is going to be a challenge."

The fourth one in Cindy's line of sight stood out from the rest. While the first three fuzzy pups clearly had a good deal of golden retriever in them, the fourth one was as furry as its siblings, except where the fur seemed to almost crinkle like a terrier. On top of that, the coloring was all wrong. Light blonde fur mixed with patches of gray and black and even a few spots here and there. Whether the father was a Spaniel or a Dalmatian or some other concoction was anyone's guess.

Grams lifted the squiggly tailwagger now noshing on her shoe. "We'd be happy to baby-sit, but we don't get much foot traffic here.

Maybe Poppy?" Grams spun around.

"She has a point." Lucy tipped her head toward Grams. "With the renovations and upcoming yard sale there are lots of folks coming and going at the church."

The little critter in Gram's arms woofed at Poppy then squirmed its way out of the older woman's embrace and almost flew at her.

"I guess he, or she, thinks that's a great idea too." Lucy handed a brown paper bag over to Poppy. "I added a little honey butter in there too. I know how Pastor Bob loves it."

"Here." Cindy handed over a small shopping bag. "She's had breakfast, but you'll have to feed her lunch and maybe an early dinner. There are also a couple of chew toys for distraction and a leash in case you go for a walk."

Poppy raised a brow at her sister. Like she'd have time to take a dog for a walk. "Thanks. And I really do have to go." Stopping dead in her tracks, puppy under one arm, bag of dog food in the other, she glanced back at her sister. "It is housebroken, isn't it?"

"We're working on it." There was nothing about Cindy's twinkling eyes and muffled chuckle that gave Poppy confidence.

Maybe this wasn't such a great idea. Redoing the church floors was proving hard enough, the last thing they needed was more sprinkling.

● ● ● ●

The town tossing a lakeside cabin into the package to convince Dylan to take on the church restoration had been unnecessary, but he was *really* glad the General had insisted. The appeal of the project on its own merits was more than enough to drag him away from his North Texas home. The draw of the lakefront property successfully exceeded his wildest expectations. Texas had plenty of lakes, but he'd yet to see one that compared with the natural beauty of this New England brook-filled body of water. Sitting on the front porch with a warm cup of coffee reminded him of his travels in Italy. Lake Como in all its famed beauty, and it was beautiful, had nothing on Hart Land.

"Good morning," Mrs. Hart called to him from the path.

"Morning." He pushed to his feet and hurried to relieve her of the large silver tray she held in her hands. He almost laughed. The rustic casual atmosphere stood out in direct contrast to the sophistication of this lovely woman and her tray. "Allow me, please."

"I know better than to argue with a gentleman." The woman had a smile that could make any man feel ten feet tall. Even though Mrs. Hart and his grandmother at first sight appeared to be polar opposites, they both held the same disarming charm that welcomed anyone into their home and made them feel they belonged. "Lucy thought if you sampled breakfast, perhaps we could coax you to join us for dinner tonight."

Setting the tray down on the round table between the two porch chairs, he lifted the corner of the cloth covering just high enough for the aroma of warm croissants to slam into him. A deep moan of delight rumbled in his throat. If they tasted half as good as they smelled, he was in for a treat.

"Lucy baked them but they're actually a batch from my granddaughter Lily's bakery." Pride shone in Mrs. Hart's eyes.

Until now he hadn't been hungry. A morning coffee man, he'd enjoy two or three cups before starting work, and would later grab an early lunch. Once he'd taken a bite of the flaky French bread, he spotted the bacon, omelet and, he suspected, fresh-squeezed orange juice. Suddenly he was famished.

"Oh, I almost forgot. The pastor called. Another box for you was delivered to the church a few minutes ago."

"Perfect." Based on the photographs and data the church board had sent him, he'd shipped most of what he should need, picked up a few more items from the local hardware store on Main Street, but as of yesterday afternoon, one box had yet to arrive. Now, he was ready to get to work. He'd been itching to see the nearly two hundred year old walls.

"Oh, fudge." A voice carried downwind.

Dylan glanced up the path. At the top of the hill, a gentleman in eyeglasses struggled to contain a couple of squirming animals. From this distance he couldn't quite make out if they were furry lambs or puppies, but he suspected that puppy was more likely.

A slim blonde shoved another wiggling creature at him and ran down the path chasing a galloping furball. "Come here, sweetie," the woman shouted seconds before scooping up what was clearly a puppy into her arms and nuzzling her nose against his fur. Just as quickly as she descended on the rambunctious critter, she turned and hurried back up the hill, hopping into the car with the gentleman and the other two puppies.

"*That* would be my granddaughter Hyacinth. We call her Cindy. She and her sister Calytrix decided at a young age that their names were too stuffy so they shortened them. Their mother took the hint naming the younger two Lily and Poppy."

Flowers. The girls were named after flowers. Interesting. Something told him Mrs. Hart's daughter did not follow in her mother's classic footsteps.

"The gentleman is Cindy's husband, Alan Peterson."

Dylan snapped his head around so fast his neck cracked. Any fan of the bestselling author Alan Peters knew the man's real last name was the longer Peterson.

Mrs. Hart chuckled. "Yes, Alan Peters is my grandson-in-law."

He blew out a sharp whistle. Peters knew how to string words together for one heck of a mystery.

"If you're interested," Mrs. Hart took a step back, "there are always autographed copies of his books at Edna's."

"Edna's?"

"Buy the Book, our little bookstore."

He nodded. No point in mentioning he had a shelf of Alan Peters hardcovers at home. The man wrote the kind of book that every time Dylan read it, he'd discover something he'd missed the time before. "I'll have to stop by."

She tipped her nose toward the tray. "You can bring the tray by on your way to church this morning."

"Will do." He nodded.

"And," she smiled wide enough to set her eyes twinkling, "shall we expect you for dinner tonight?"

"That would be very nice. Thank you." Normally he liked to go to bed early and rise early. This gave him time for a good night's sleep and slow and steady start to his day with a nice long run before he had to step into creative mode. But if the housekeeper cooked dinner as well as she did breakfast, he could learn to stay up a little later. Besides, perhaps someone else in the family could help him find the hat lady.

CHAPTER FOUR

"I don't know about this." Pastor Bob held the squirmy pup in his arms and scratched under the animal's chin. "There's an awful lot of energy wound up in here."

"I know." In the short drive from Hart Land to the church, the pup had managed to scramble from side to side in the back seat and then over the console and into the front seat and back. Fortunately, the little squirt waited until Poppy had pulled into the parking lot to fly into her lap. "I thought if I kept my door closed we could at least contain the energy to a fifteen by fifteen space and away from the workers."

"Not if Brent is finishing up these walls today." His head tipped to one side, the pastor smiled and set the girl down on the floor. "Does she have a name?"

"No." She shook her head, quickly rethinking what to do with the puppy for the day. "I suppose whoever adopts her should name her."

Pastor Bob nodded. "Makes sense. I'm going to be in my office for most of the morning. I have back to back appointments scheduled. One is with the insurance adjuster."

"Again?" She had no idea what was the point of carrying insurance if winning a Nobel Prize was easier than getting a claim paid.

"Again," he sighed.

She really did hope guardian angels existed and that one was battling the insurance company on the pastor's behalf. The creases across his forehead were growing deeper and she didn't like it. If the tight pull on Mrs. Sullivan's smile every time she stopped by was any sign, his wife didn't like the insurance company much either.

"Whoa." Tool belt in hand, Brent came to a fast stop at the doorway in front of the bundle of energy now galloping circles around him. "Where did you come from?"

"Mrs. Nashua's golden had a litter. She needs a home."

Up on its hind legs, its front paws flat against Brent's chest, the puppy was having a great time cleaning Brent's face. On his knees, eyes and mouth tightly closed, Brent didn't seem to be having too bad a time himself.

"Isn't that sweet," Poppy practically cooed. "She seems to be very fond of you."

"Oh, no." Brent nudged the puppy back, scratched behind one ear, and shook his head. "I live in an apartment. Dogs are meant for backyards."

"Lots of people have dogs in apartments."

"Not dogs with paws like that." Brent waved an extended finger in the direction of the puppy now batting about a crumpled ball of paper.

So distracted by the kaleidoscope of colors, textures, and the boundless energy, she hadn't actually taken note of the paws. Brent was right. When the body caught up with the feet, this was going to be one big pup. "I guess they are a little on the large side."

Still grinning, Brent nodded. "Don't be surprised if papa turns out to be an Irish wolfhound."

Poppy's head snapped around. If her memory served her correctly, Irish wolfhounds were as big as Great Danes, who were as big as small horses. For her own conscience, she'd have to do her best to make sure whichever parishioner fell in love with this funky looking mutt better have a backyard big enough to match those paws.

"What's on the itinerary for today?" she asked.

Brent snapped his belt on. "Sheet rock goes up in here. Then the drywall compound. Tomorrow will hopefully be the paint, and lastly reinstall the salvaged wainscoting. It'll be easier that way if we don't have to be as careful with the paint."

Normally a project like this was done in layers. All the sheetrock in the building repaired, then floated, then painted. Since for now, besides the floor guys, there were no crews, only Brent and volunteers helping as time permitted, the decision was made to work one section at a time, starting with offices so no one would have to work day in and day out looking at the disrepair. "I'm so glad it wasn't damaged and that you can re-do it."

"You can thank your grandfather for that. The man ran the volunteer crew like… well, a general." Brent laughed at the irony of his own words. "The General knew where to focus to avoid the most damage. If the carpets had stayed down to fully dry after the water was sucked up, there's no telling how bad it would have been."

"I'm just glad it wasn't any worse."

"You and me both."

"I almost forgot to mention." Pastor Bob poked his head into the room. "When Mr. Powell arrives this morning, tell him yesterday's box is in the janitor's closet. Seemed the only spot that isn't in some kind of upheaval."

"Got it."

The pastor tapped the door frame with the back of his wedding ring and retreated to his office.

"This is the guy who's coming all the way from Texas?" Brent asked.

Poppy nodded. "We were quite fortunate to get him. Some of the board of directors felt that the church couldn't afford to take on such a project at this time, but others felt the soot covered art would be a depressing sight for the congregation to be subjected to week after week."

"I suppose they have a point. They're going to need every dime the tag sale generates."

"Tell me about it." Few people knew just how significantly the church had been tightening its belt and for how long. "At least Mr. McGuire didn't have his way. He didn't see any reason why you couldn't just take a brush and dish soap to the mural and clean it off ourselves."

Luscious green eyes almost rolled back in Brent's head. "Just when I think people can no longer surprise me, someone steps up to the plate and swings."

Poppy muffled a laugh. She felt that way more often than she should.

"We're going to have to come to an agreement." Brent scooped the puppy into his arms. "I hammer in sheetrock, you play in the opposite side of the room."

"Oh my." Shoving the chair back and standing up, Poppy

marched to the doorway. "This good deed is proving to be harder than I expected."

"Good deed?"

"Helping show the gal off to find a permanent home." Sliding her arm around the pup's midsection, she slid the pup away from Brent and swung around, slamming into an immoveable force. One that didn't belong in the entry. "Sorry."

The puppy woofed, wagged its tail with the velocity of a metronome on steroids and pushing hard on Poppy's forearms, leapt into the unsuspecting arms of the tall-as-a-tree visitor.

"Hey there." Smothering his arms around the puppy and taking a step back, the stranger showed great reflexes. His balance wasn't bad either.

Retreating a step herself, Poppy's eyes followed a trail from the puppy in two nicely tanned arms, up a chest she could now see was wide and firm, further up strong corded neck muscles, past a squarely chiseled chin, and stuttered to a stop at a smile that made her heart skip a beat. Not till her gaze leveled with two brown eyes twinkling with merriment did her heart stop all together. *Him.*

• • • •

After breakfast this morning, as far as Dylan was concerned, the day couldn't get any better. Or so he thought. Scratching behind the ears of the scraggliest downright ugly yet adorable puppy he'd ever seen, Dylan couldn't believe the hat lady was standing in front of him. "Hello."

In a flash her expression went from soft and worried to fire, and he strongly suspected not in a good way either. Like flipping a switch, in another instant, her gaze dropped and she slid long slim fingers around the sides of the puppy. "Sorry. Let me take her."

Before she could get a grip on the animal, the pup rotated onto her back, giving Dylan easier access to her chin and promptly nodded off to sleep. "Isn't it something how they can do that? Be a bundle of energy one second and drop off sound asleep where they stand the next."

The woman's fingers froze as she gazed down on the profoundly sleeping dog.

"Good work," a man a few feet away remarked, nodding his approval.

It took Dylan a few seconds to realize the guy was referring to the puppy sleeping.

Poppy's big brown eyes lifted to meet his. Glistening softly with—was that admiration? "How'd you do that?"

"I wish I could tell you the secret but puppies, like kittens and even children, when they play hard, they collapse hard. It's Mother Nature. I can't take the credit." Not that he didn't sorely want to if it meant her eyes would never again shoot daggers at him.

"I should take him." The way she nibbled on her lower lip, he could tell that disturbing the sleeping animal was actually the last thing she wanted to do.

"I've got her. She won't nap long. They recharge quickly."

"That's what I'm afraid of," she muttered under her breath, taking a few steps back. "How may I help you?"

"I'm Dylan Powell."

Once again, her eyes flew open. "The art conservator?"

"Last time I checked." A broad smile did little to coax a cheerful response from her. "And you are?"

"Poppy Nelson. I'm the pastor's assistant."

Poppy. A flower. Surely there weren't two young women in town with that name? "Nice to meet you."

The fellow who had been standing nearby stuck his hand out. "Brent Mitchell. I'll be working around the church here and there. Just let me know if I disturb you in any way."

"No problem. I'm used to working with quite a bit of chaos around me." His gaze swept over the small office. Considering how recent the fire had been, the condition was surprisingly neat. The working desk for the pretty hat lady was both neat and organized. Stacks of paintings rested against the window seat. While the walls showed signs of recent fire damage, the windows were shiny and clean. He was impressed. Then he saw it. "Sweet."

Puppy in his arms, Dylan crossed the room to the far wall perpendicular to the windows and the desk. Even covered in the residue of the fire, it was still a stunning piece. Wrongly, he'd assumed all the work would be religious of nature. Perhaps a last supper or prayers in the garden. A landscape had not occurred to him.

"Isn't it amazing?" For the first time in his presence, a smile graced the young lady's lips.

His gaze searched for a signature. "Any idea who painted this?"

"Rumor has it that when Frederic Church was traveling around New England sketching, the beauty of the lake enthralled him so that he painted that for the church."

"Rumor?" Dylan stepped forward. The style did indeed resemble that of Church but somehow raw, bolder. Perhaps that of a young man not quite mastered in his own style. Or, the work of another gifted nineteenth century painter. "No corroboration?"

She shook her head. "I'm afraid not."

Regardless, it would still be a delight to restore the wonderful work.

"Would you like to see the rest of the murals?"

"Yes, thank you." Right about now he'd follow her into the bowels of hell. Odd. He'd met more than a fair share of beautiful women. Knockouts by anyone's standards. Blondes, brunettes, redheads, even a color chart of colors, but not a single one stuck so firmly in his mind. Now all he had to figure out was what do to about it.

CHAPTER FIVE

"Would you be any relation to the Harts?" Puppy still perfectly ensconced in the crook of his arm, the wall of a man followed behind her.

"Yes, as a matter of fact. General Hart is my grandfather."

A wry smile teased at his lips. He had a very nice smile. Too nice. "I had a feeling."

"Why is that?" With dark hair and dark eyes and a heart-shaped face, she tended to take after her dad's side of the family.

"At breakfast this morning, Mrs. Hart mentioned her granddaughters by name."

"Ah." She should have known. By now someone at Hart House had most likely told him everything about her and her sisters' short of their shoe sizes. Then again, they might have disclosed that as well.

"It's a lovely name." His gaze had lifted to the ceilings.

"Thank you." As they crossed the main portion of the church to the largest mural with, she hoped, the least amount of damage, she glanced over her shoulder. The nameless puppy was still out like the proverbial light, but this man was fully enthralled with the ceilings above. Not slowing down, she lifted her gaze to the ceilings as well. The old beams were hundreds of years old but they were, well, beams. She much preferred the beauty of the different paintings, both murals and framed. The church really did have some extraordinary artwork for a small congregation in a mountain town. "Here you go."

Dylan's gaze dropped from the ceiling to the wall in front of them. His eyes widened ever so slightly. Not so much with surprise, but with what struck her as raw delight.

"It's one of my favorites."

"And barely touched." His lips lifted into a satisfied smile. "This will be easy."

She almost laughed. Maybe for him.

His gaze slowly covered the entire expanse of the precious

wall. Bobbing his head slowly, his fingers still caressing the underside of the puppy's chin, he turned away, taking in the remainder of the church. "When you think about the limited tools available two hundred years ago, and you see these beautiful results, it's almost miraculous."

"I'd never really given much thought to how this church was built, but I do agree there isn't the craftsmanship there once was." Changing direction, she waved him forward with her finger. "There's one more. This one got the brunt of the smoke and the water and all the efforts to put the fire out."

Dylan failed to mask his grimace. Taking in a deep breath, he turned to her. "The good news is this piece was not fully destroyed by the fire. You can't restore ashes. At least we have something to work with."

"I was so hoping you were going to say that. Nobody was willing to voice the words, but we were all concerned that this one was too far gone."

His gaze seemed to zero in on one corner. "Have you had dehumidifiers running in here?"

"We have. The water extractors were called immediately. The parishioners were able to extract a good deal of the water before the professionals arrived with the heavy machinery, including the dehumidifiers."

"Good." The tiniest hint of a smile touched his lips. "I'll know more once I start working, but it sounds like you did everything right."

"I certainly hope so."

As if bored with the direction of the conversation, the puppy snapped alert, squirming in Dylan's arms. Turning herself upright, the now rejuvenated canine woofed happily and paws on Dylan's shoulders, licked his face. The urge to smile overtook any lingering irritation with this man. The puppy's delight combined with this man's scrunched expression as he let the furball lick his face with the gusto of a starving man given a rib eye steak, would have been enough to make any grouch smile.

Was there anything as entertaining as a rambunctious puppy? Footsteps fell behind them and intrigued with the sounds, the little dog quickly lost interest in Dylan's face and wiggled out of his arms.

"Uh oh." Poppy turned quickly on her heel.

"Who knew something with such short legs could move so fast." Dylan hurried beside her.

Sliding across the wooden floors more than she ran, the little puppy skidded smack into the pastor's shoes.

"Now why aren't I surprised to find you here?" No matter what, Pastor Bob always managed to find the humor in just about any situation.

"I'm so sorry." Poppy came to a stop beside the pastor.

"I'm afraid it's my fault," Dylan said. "I should have had a tighter grip on her."

"And you are?" Pastor reached down to pick up the puppy only to have it bolt toward the open front doors.

"Oh, dear." Poppy heaved a sigh. "Here we go again."

"I'm Dylan Powell." Not waiting for pleasantries, he darted after the puppy, calling out his answer over his shoulder. "He really does have speed on his side."

The little fellow pranced past the painters at the front door and without slowing down, bit down on the handle of a paint brush resting atop a can, and kept going.

Dylan sucked in an audible breath. "That can't be good."

Rump wagging at the same speed as her tail, semi gloss white paint dripping from the bristles, and one startled painter scrambling behind them, the puppy seemed to still be somehow smiling up at them.

"That is my best brush for cutting in," the unhappy painter muttered.

Dylan glanced left then right, slowly inching toward the puppy. No doubt wondering the same thing she was. How do you get a wet paint brush away from an excited puppy without getting splattered with semi-gloss paint? Reaching over to one side of the railing, he grabbed a decent sized branch, snapped it in two, stripped most of the leaves off, and hunching down, he waved the quickly made toy in front of the dog. "Come here, sweetie. Look what I have for you."

The puppy's ears seemed to stiffen at the same time her head tipped to one side.

"That's it. This is much more fun than that dirty old paintbrush." Dylan continued to inch closer to the puppy, his gaze darting off to the street and back.

Taking his lead, Poppy squatted lower to the ground.

Within grabbing distance, he swished the leafy side of the branch in front of the puppy. The little gal's head tipped the other way and in a simultaneously smooth move, Dylan's right hand tugged the brush away and his left hand held the chewable end of the twig at puppy mouth level.

"Bravo." Poppy scooped the puppy up and pushed to her feet. "Very well done."

"I figured the same principles that apply to my toddler nephew probably would apply to a toddler dog."

"Nonetheless, very well done."

"Or very lucky, but glad to help." His gaze darted back to the office. "But this does pose a problem. Once I unpack I'm going to have way more supplies to draw her interest than just a wet paint brush."

"I think puppies are above my pay grade."

"I think puppies are above most people's pay grade." Reaching out to scratch the puppy behind his ears, Dylan raised his eyes to meet hers. "Know anyone with an older playpen?"

Playpen? Oh. Playpen. "You seem to be batting a thousand today. That's a great idea. I'm going to call my grandmother. If anyone can find me a spare playpen in a hurry, it's her or Lucy. Those two are amazing."

Dylan nodded. Poppy trotted to her office, puppy in arms, and for a flash of a moment, she felt a pang of envy that this sweet puppy had been able to snuggle up close to a man she'd barely met. How ridiculous was that?

• • • •

While Poppy hurried into her office in search of something to help contain all that puppy energy, Dylan was thankful he had not unloaded everything from his trunk last night. At the time he'd gone hunting in the shops on Main Street he'd thought his idea a good one.

Even when he'd tucked his purchase safely into the backseat of the car, he'd still been confident in the idea. Now, standing outside the church by his car, staring up at the big old building, picturing the gentle brunette inside, well, now he wasn't so sure.

The goal had been to make her happy. To make up for his clod-footed mistake. Except yesterday the sadness in the unsettled woman's eyes had pricked his conscience. Today those same eyes had warmed his heart, and the notion of making things between them worse not better scared the bejeezus out of him. Not even in high school when he was more hormones and high hopes than good sense had he been this torn over a gift for a woman.

"Suck it up, buster." Like it or not, he couldn't stand outside all day long. He needed to make up his mind and needed to make it up now. This is ridiculous. He was not an awkward teen, he was a grown man. A man whose instincts had done him well through the years. Straightening his shoulders, he made up his mind. "Here goes nothing."

He barely made it a few steps when, puppy in arms, Poppy came flying down the church steps. Dashing past him, she paused just long enough to explain she was on her way somewhere to pick up a porta-something. He could only guess it had something to do with containing the puppy and not toilets for construction.

"Be back in a jiffy." Her smile wide and bright, Poppy plopped the pup in the backseat and sliding behind the wheel, she was off and pulling onto the main road.

The shopping bag in one hand, he slammed his car door and clicking the fob, even though he doubted this small town had an issue with crime, he took the church steps two at a time. Inside, the contractor was screwing sheetrock onto the wall and Dylan realized he had no idea where any of the things he'd shipped ahead were. As a matter of fact, as he looked around, he wondered where would be the best place to start without getting in everyone's way.

The buzz of the power drill slowed to a stop and the contractor turned to face him. "Pastor Bob is in the janitor's closet retrieving your shipments."

"Oh, good." He turned toward the doorway.

Drill in hand, Brent waved his arm. "At the end of the hall. It's the first door on the left after the sanctuary."

"Got it. Thanks." Before he crossed the threshold, the pastor appeared in front of him, box in arms.

"I'm not sure where Poppy put your other packages." Pastor Bob leaned the small box against the desk. "Where do you want to start?"

The question should have been where *should* he start? Easily the large mural in the main church would make the most sense. The possible Church painted mural held the most intrigue, not so much because of the artist but its placement in the same area as Poppy's desk.

"I'm almost done installing the sheetrock here. The next step isn't as noisy. If you want to start on that wall I shouldn't disturb you." The contractor's gaze shifted over to Poppy's desk and back. "She hasn't been her usual self since the fire. Can't help but think the sooner this place gets back to normal the sooner we'll have all of her back."

Dylan wondered what part of her was missing, but didn't dare pry. The thing was, so far she seemed pretty complete to him. Not one to look a gift horse in the mouth, he nodded at Brent, grateful for a good excuse to do exactly what he wanted even if it wasn't necessarily the most practical. "Then I guess we start in here."

For the most part, despite the remnants of chaos anyone would expect to find after a fire of this type, there seemed plenty of room for him to set up without disturbing the daily routine of the church office. Even the paintings that he presumed came from the wall Brent was repairing were neatly stacked across the room. One in particular had caught his eye. A corner exposed to the light of the window, he pushed the Orthodox Madonna out of the natural light. Finding a piece of Orthodox artwork in a western church wasn't that common, but something more than the eastern-western contrast seemed out of place. He just couldn't quite put his finger on it.

"I'm back." Poppy swept into the room, her long skirt billowing around her legs. "I either need someone to help with the furball or the playpen. Any volunteers?"

"At your disposal." Dylan waved an arm and bent at the waist.

Brent set his drill down. "I'm in too."

In a matter of only a few minutes, the three had set up the mesh pen just outside the doorway. Close enough to keep an eye on the pup, but far enough into the main building that anyone not coming into Poppy's office couldn't miss spotting her. The first thirty minutes or so had been spent settling the pup down. As long as someone stood nearby she was content. The minute anyone returned to the other room to work, the little gal would raise a fuss. Not till he thought to ask one of the painters for an old brush did the puppy find a toy worthy of entertaining her.

"Before you settle into work," Dylan cleared his throat and pulled the paper shopping bag from beside Poppy's desk, "there's something I'd like you to have."

Her eyes lit with interest. If he were a betting man he'd wager she enjoyed surprises.

"It's not exactly the same," he muttered as she slid the tissue clad gift from the bag. Slowly she lifted the tissue paper away. Poppy wasn't one to rip through a gift, but clearly savored every moment, appreciated the journey as much as the destination. A person could tell a lot about someone by the way they opened gifts, but right now he kept his gaze on hers, waiting for some glimmer of a reaction. Another sheet of paper and the wide brimmed replacement was in full view.

"It's a hat," she said softly, turning it carefully about in her hands. "It's… beautiful."

"I know it's a little different, but I'd hoped…" his words trailed off. He wasn't sure what he'd hoped other than that the replacement would make her happy.

Her gaze still focused on the gift, he couldn't really see her reaction and then it hit him. Right in the solar plexus. Beautiful big brown eyes looked up at him. Her entire face was lit with delight. "I love it. It's my new favorite." Right away she placed it on her head and tipped her chin up then down, left then right, then back again.

If the hat was her new favorite, then the other must have been the original favorite. Even though she seemed to truly love the replacement, he still felt horrible for nearly destroying the original. Somehow he didn't feel the relief he'd expected. There was no reassurance that he'd paid his debt. "Do you get a lunch hour?"

Her head popped up from her desk. "Doesn't everyone?"

"I suppose." He smiled. "I guess the better question would have been do you take a lunch hour?"

"I do. Both." Her smile truly took over her face.

"Good." He shuffled in place. Nothing like diving right into a lunchtime invitation without a clue of the options they had. "I'd be happy if you'd let me take you to lunch. Another thank you for not running me out of town on a rail yesterday."

"Thank you, but I don't know that I dare leave the puppy here alone, and I know Mabel would not appreciate a puppy at the diner."

"Of course." He hoped his disappointment didn't show. "Don't know what I was thinking."

"You could go to the One Stop," Brent suggested between drill runs.

"One Stop?" he asked.

"Best lobster rolls on the Eastern seaboard," Brent provided. "Katie has a nice little outdoor set up during the warm season."

He didn't dare say a word, instead he did his best to read Poppy's expression.

"You know," her smile brightened even more, "if there's anyone in town who can teach this gal a thing or two, it's Katie."

Yes! He had a date for lunch in…the time on his watch said 11:50 am. Where had the morning gone? "Shall we go now, or wait a bit longer?"

"Now. The sooner we teach little mixed mutt here how to behave, the sooner this will all be over with."

He hadn't made up his mind about the puppy yet, but he did know something else for sure. He was not ready for anything involving Poppy Nelson to be over. Not yet.

CHAPTER SIX

T he One Stop had been a staple on Lawford Mountain for as long as Poppy could remember. That included Katie, and her grandmother before her.

"Well, this is a lovely afternoon surprise." Standing behind the counter, Katie smiled up at Poppy as she and Dylan came through the front door, and hurried around to greet them—and of course the tail wagging pup.

"I haven't had enough chance to come enjoy your special lobster rolls." Returning the bright Irish smile was easy for Poppy. Katie had a way of making everyone a little happier than they'd been a moment before. Some folks even teased she was a Fey or a leprechaun, while others firmly believed she was simply an angel.

"If you be asking me now, they work you too hard at that church. Someone should have a sit down with Pastor Bob and let him know that somebody as young as you needs to have some free time to enjoy the brief summertime. Heaven knows it passes by too fast." A stern glance in Poppy's direction shifted to twinkling eyes at Dylan, all the while one finger scratching the under the oddly submissive puppy's chin. "And who might these two be?"

"Dylan Powell, our restoration specialist. And this little gal is one of four looking for a home." Poppy waved an arm from Dylan and the puppy in his arms to Katie. "Everyone's favorite shopkeeper, Katie O'Leary."

"Pleased to meet you." Katie extended her hand.

"All mine, I'm sure." The sincere smile exposed two perfectly placed dimples.

"I'm sure this unique little one will have no trouble finding a home." Straightening her shoulders and taking a step back, Katie looked from one to the other. "Now is it two lobster roll lunches or are we feeding the little one too?"

"Just two," Poppy said. "Please."

"Very well. Help yourselves to whatever you'd be drinking and then have your pick of tables outside. Don't let the little one roam too far, we are in the woods after all."

With a nod and a wave, she and Dylan each grabbed a soda and securing the edge of the leash under a chair leg, settled in at the table closest to the wall of trees.

"I keep thinking the views can't get any better, and then something goes and surprises me."

"I am awfully lucky to have been raised so close to heaven."

"Great way to phrase it. Close to heaven."

The dog kept herself distracted, slowly sniffing every square inch of every surface within the leash's reach.

"Looks like bringing her here was a good idea." Dylan smiled down at the puppy. His gaze shifted from the small animal, pausing briefly on the lake in the distance, before settling his attention on her. "I'm so glad you liked the hat."

Instinctively she reached up and adjusted the brim slightly.

"I can't tell you how awful I felt when I realized that I stomped not once, but twice, on your hat."

"It wasn't important."

"Yes, it was. I could see it in your eyes."

She fingered the plastic silverware Katie had set out for them. "I'd had the hat a long time. Wearing it always made me feel like I'd been transported to a wild flower field in a distant land on a summer day."

"Not here on the mountain?"

She shook her head. She loved the mountain very much, but sometimes she dreamed of places far away and very different from, well, here. "I would think it might be nice to visit a hillside in Scotland or Ireland, or maybe Austria."

"I can tell you none of those places have anything on this mountain. Especially not Austria, they look almost the same. As for Scotland or Ireland, those warm sunny days are usually accompanied by a good deal of rain. Are you a fan of rainy days?"

"Not enough to build another ark, while a nice change of pace. I gather you have been to all those places?"

He nodded. "Didn't have time to do a great deal of tourism, but

I've done a lot of study abroad. In my business, many of the true masters at older, really older, artwork are simply not here."

"I suppose that makes sense. If you wanted to learn how to restore precious works from the dynasties of China, you'd be unlikely to study treasures in Texas."

His sudden burst of laughter almost made her giddy. "Let's agree that I'd probably learn more in the *treasures'* homeland."

"And here you go." Katie appeared quietly beside them setting two plates of her famed sandwiches along with some home fried potato chips. "I brought a little something for our four-footed friend."

Anyone would've thought the dog spoke English. At Katie's mention of the four-footed friend, her intense interest in her surroundings and the nearby brick path instantly faded.

Katie held out a beef jerky dog treat. A brief moment of caution preceded the puppy happily snatching it from her fingers and curling up at Dylan's feet with it.

"I'd say you scored a few brownie points." Dylan reached over to scratch behind the puppy's ears as she chewed on the beef stick trapped between her front paws.

"Katie doesn't need brownie points. Animals love her."

"Well now, look at that." Katie smiled down at the now sleeping puppy. There wasn't anyone in town who had the same way with animals as Katie, not even Cindy, but this man seemed to have the magic touch when it came to putting a rambunctious puppy to sleep. "You've got the gift. You'll make a good father some day."

"I don't know that I had anything to do with her falling asleep."

"Hm." Katie seemed to disagree, but silently turned just as a car pulled into the lot. "I'd better go tend to my other customers."

Two hands on the massive sandwich and Poppy bit back a laugh at how wide Dylan had to open his mouth to take the first bite. The man swallowed hard and whistled. "Oh, man this is good."

"Better." Unlike her companion, she slowly nibbled on the edges, working her way in. She took her time relishing a good thing. This was one of the few chances she'd had to come sample Katie's summer menu and she was going to enjoy every single bite.

Leaning forward to let crumbs fall on the paper plate, her gaze lifted to the man across from her and the long slender fingers gripping the last half of his sandwich. The hands of an artist.

One hand abandoned his sandwich and an extended finger swiped at his mouth. "Am I making a mess?"

She swallowed quickly. "What?"

"You're looking at me like I'm drooling."

"Oh." Setting the sandwich down, she dabbed at her mouth with a paper napkin. "I'm sorry, I was just thinking you have the hands of an artist."

That dimple inducing smile reappeared. "My grandmother says that all the time."

"Then I must be right."

He shrugged. "I'm not a Picasso or Rembrandt, but I do dabble."

"Dabble?"

"Occasionally, I pick up a paint brush for pleasure. Recently I painted my grandmother and my sister's children for an upcoming birthday gift."

"If your grandmother is anything like mine, she's going to love it."

His smile widened. "I think she'd love stick figures if I gave it to her, but I'm hoping it makes her happy."

Taking another bite of her sandwich, she did her best to discreetly study this man. Caring—after all, he'd replaced her hat on his own. Good with animals—he'd put the puppy to sleep. Had a killer smile to match twinkling gray eyes. Yep, for now she was going to enjoy her lunch and especially enjoy the view.

●　●　●　●

"Have I told you how much I love the smell of chocolate in this kitchen?" Poppy crossed into the heart of the house. The afternoon had flown by. Something about having a good-looking man working within feet of a girl's desk just made the day a little brighter. Even if one was merely a good friend and the other was virtually a stranger.

Cindy nudged the puppy into the crate. Apparently she'd learned her lesson transporting the bundles of energy around town. "Lucy's on a Depression cake roll."

Depression cake? Uh oh.

"It just isn't right." Lucy, the family housekeeper who was more family than employee, slapped the dirty cake pan in the kitchen sink and turned on the water. "Such a nice, pretty girl."

"She does look a bit low." Fiona Hart stood over the box of modeling clay and leftover fabrics she'd be donating to charity.

"Low?" Lucy squirted dish soap on the two pans. "She's scraping the floor."

"Who is?" The back door clicked shut and Callie dropped a stack of books on the island.

Poppy did her best to signal her sister with a pointed glare not to go down that road.

"The guest in the Hickory cabin." Lucy scrubbed the soaking tray. Hard.

"Poor thing." Grams shook her head. "Thought she was going to be proposed to."

"Depression cake?" Callie snatched a piece of Lucy's beloved chocolate cake, popped it into her mouth, and Poppy would have sworn her eyes rolled back in her head.

"Thought?" Cindy stood and swiped a piece of the cake.

Why was Cindy encouraging Lucy to focus on the not-engaged guest? Did having a fiancé of her own actually deaden Cindy's matchmaking radar? Could she not see that Lucy, their own self-declared Dolly Levy, was setting herself up to play matchmaker to this unsuspecting woman and some as yet unknown unsuspecting man? For some people, being set up on a date could prove to be a great thing, but not when it involved Lucy. Her efforts only succeeded in creating bedlam for everyone involved. And if this woman was at the lake, as sure as the sun rises, someone on Hart Land was bound to get caught in the inevitable mishap.

"From what we can tell—" Grams started.

"Between the tears." Lucy cut her employer off and slapped more furiously at the cake pan. "She'd learned all about football so they could watch games together."

Callie and Cindy looked away from the cake to Lucy and then Poppy.

Finally, she gave her two siblings that wide-eyed *think before you open your mouth* glare. It was useless; these two would soon be in a chocolate cake coma.

"And," her grandmother added, "his family is Portuguese. She learned to speak Portuguese."

Callie lifted her brows high on her forehead. "I'm impressed."

For the first time since the conversation started, Lucy looked up from the sink and, noticing the dwindling size of her baked goods, reached out, lightly smacking each sister. "Save some for guest in the Birchcabin."

"Is he joining us for dinner?" Callie asked another piece of cake in her hand. The old family recipe was a favorite and one that Lucy didn't make often.

"Yes, he is." Lucy froze mid sentence. A familiar gleam in her eye.

Oh no. "If the restoration work today is any example of what's to come, I'm sure Dylan is going to be working a lot of long hours. He'll probably want to be early to bed and skip dessert."

Lucy let out a long sigh and returned to scrubbing what was already a clean pan. Mr. Powell was going to owe her one for saving him from some matchmaking collision with the guest in the Hickory cabin, apparently crying a waterfall.

The front door creaked, announcing another arrival.

"You'd better mix up another cake." Grams pointed to the one plate that had already been scarfed up by the sisters.

"Did I hear cake?" Dylan walked into the kitchen.

For a fraction in time, Poppy felt her breath catch. The unexpected reaction made her feel like a teen crushing on the captain of the football team. Only she wasn't a teen, she was well past the age of infatuation on sight, and even though this project could take months, eventually he would be going home. Nope, she was going to have to get a grip on her inner teenager. And fast.

• • • •

"Lucy is baking her grandmother's recipe for Depression cake."

It took Dylan a few seconds to process the information. The only conclusion he could come to was that someone must be depressed. "So we're trying to cheer someone up?"

"Actually," Grams chuckled, "we are. But that's not why it's called Depression cake."

Lucy scooped flour into a bowl. "The recipe doesn't require eggs, butter or milk. All ingredients hard to find during the Depression."

"I see."

"Don't let the ingredients, or lack of, scare you. It's always delicious."

Mrs. Hart had no idea how funny that statement was. If she'd told him the recipe called for mustard and collard greens, he'd have assumed it was going to be delicious. As his grandmother would say when she knew nothing of a subject, what he knew about baking wouldn't fill a thimble. "I'm sure it's delicious."

Wiping a wayward crumb from the corner of her mouth, Poppy grinned up at him. "It seriously is."

An image of his hand stretching out and wiping that crumb away popped to mind and he had to clench his fists at his side to stop from doing just that. Shifting his attention away from temptation, he scanned the room, taking in all the new faces.

"Here, try a piece, if you promise not to let it spoil your dinner." Mrs. Hart handed him a dish with the aforementioned cake, then turned to wave at the others. "Have you met my granddaughters, Callie and Cindy?"

"How do you do?"

"I'm Cindy, the one with the puppies." She motioned toward a crate with a cluster of furballs snuggled together.

"I'm Callie." Another blonde, this one in jeans and sporting a ponytail, stretched out her hand.

"Nice to meet you all."

"Oh, we're not all." Cindy laughed.

Callie swallowed the last bite of cake and wiping her hands at her sides, nodded. "Yep. We're nine all together and you're bound to meet us all before you leave."

"Hey." Another granddaughter, this one a redhead with the same killer smile as Poppy, came through the door. "Who started a party without me?"

"That's Lily."

Waving a few fingers at him, her eyes popped open and she snatched up the last piece of cake in the pan.

So far he'd met almost half the granddaughters, and not an ugly one in the bunch. But not a single one drew him in the way Poppy did. His gaze drifted to where she sat, laughing at something the redhead had whispered in her ear. If he was going to be living and working with her for the duration of this restoration, he was going to have to get a grip. Her nose crinkled as she let out another burst of laughter and his fingers curled once again into his palms. There were several unspoken codes of honor among men. Never mess with a buddy's sister was at the top of the list. Every military man knew never to mess with a superior officer's daughter—or granddaughter. What wasn't so clear was did his grandfather's buddy count, and did it matter if the superior officer wasn't his?

CHAPTER SEVEN

"" ow are things going?"

"Not bad." Harold Hart thought back to last night on the front porch. Dylan had played cards with the men while Poppy helped her grandmother sort through donation boxes nearby. Neither said much to each other; if anything, it almost looked as if they were intentionally keeping their distance, but he caught the occasional glance. He'd have to keep a close eye on this one.

"I suppose it's too soon to expect anything else."

"We've got plenty of time this round."

"I know. I'm just ready."

Didn't he know it? A little over a year ago he was perfectly content to wait for his girls to find their own soulmate in their own time. One diagnosis later and time suddenly felt in short supply. Waiting no longer seemed like a good idea. Now, the future seemed much brighter. His final match was slowly lining up. That thought brought a smile to his lips. "Tomorrow's another day. I just might have to pop by the church." After all, progress, even slow, is still progress.

• • • •

"Good morning, General." Pastor Bob almost bumped into Harold as he crossed through the doorway of the church. "Here to see the progress or decided to take that puppy home for good?"

"Morning, Bob. Sarge and Lady are enough for us. There's a family just right for that little gal." His gaze quickly surveyed the immediate area, taking brief notice of Poppy at her desk just the other side of the puppy playpen. "Looks like things are coming together well."

"They are. I don't think I'd considered, though, how meticulous cleaning artwork would be."

"I can only imagine."

"I also didn't know there were so many sized toothbrushes."

"Toothbrushes?"

"Well, I'm sure that's not exactly what they are, but he's working painstakingly slow in one corner."

He bobbed his head. "Precise. Careful. Good, good."

"I was just on my way out, unless you need me for anything…" He let his words hang.

"No. You can be on your way. The restoration committee is having a meeting tonight. I'm going to take a few minutes to walk around to report."

Pastor Bob nodded. "Take your time."

Now he would have to remember to call the committee together for a meeting tonight. Half of them would be at the house playing cards anyhow, this way he'd make it official.

From where he stood he didn't have to move far to have a nice view into the room. Eager to simply observe, he took his time studying freshly waxed floors and neatly scrubbed pews. From the corner of his eye he could see Dylan carefully working on the wall and Poppy studiously shuffling papers at her desk. The quiet stage. Very well.

His granddaughter blew out the quietest of sighs before pushing to her feet. "I think I need more caffeine. I'm going to get a pop out of the fridge in the kitchen. Would you like something?"

Dylan straightened his back, brush still in hand, and flashed a face splitting smile in her direction. "Thank you. That would be nice."

A broad smile to bookend his took over her face. "One pop coming up."

Harold quickly retreated into the vestibule. Progress, even slow, was progress.

• • • •

For the first time in a long time, Fiona sat on the porch simply reading a book. The sight caught Harold off guard. Usually by the end of breakfast, his beautiful wife was deeply into her latest new craft. "No new project?"

Deep blue eyes, pearly white teeth, and rosy cheeks lifted to face him. All these years and she was as beautiful as ever. Both inside and out. "Have I mentioned lately how much I love you and our life together?"

The blue eyes sparkled with delight. "Not in the last hour or so."

Just as he leaned over to gently kiss her cheek, laughter caught his attention. Halfway between his daughter Virginia and Poppy's cabin, and the Birch cabin where Dylan stayed, Poppy and Dylan were corralling the puppy.

"Cindy dropped her off this morning. She had to make a run out of town early this morning for an injured horse and couldn't wait for Poppy to get to work."

"Wonder what they're going to do with the pup tomorrow. Or is Poppy planning on working Saturdays now?"

"I think I heard Dylan say he was going to work on the restoration tomorrow. I don't know about Poppy."

"Hm." The sight before him was much improved over yesterday at the church. Not tasked with a job to do, the two were laughing and talking with animated gestures. The puppy danced circles around their feet, drawing more fervent laughter, with Dylan tossing the occasional ball to her.

"He picked up a few dog toys yesterday and is teaching the puppy to fetch."

Just then Dylan held the ball and the pup's rear plopped on the ground. "And to sit."

"And to sit." Fiona nodded. "He's quite good with the puppy. Patient but firm. Good qualities in a man."

"Or a Marine." What neither of them said aloud was husband and father. Yes. Progress, even slow, was progress.

● ● ● ●

"Our guest in the Hickory cabin is extending her stay. She was supposed to be here for the balloon fest this weekend but says she wants to stay on for the big church yard sale coming up." Wiping her hands on her apron, Lucy set a fresh pitcher of lemonade in the fridge. "Personally, I think she just doesn't want to go home and face her friends and family without a fiancé."

Harold knew better than to touch that comment with a ten-foot pole. He glanced at his watch. Almost six pm and no sign of his granddaughter or Dylan. Actually, for a Saturday, the house was amazingly quiet. "Where is everyone?"

"Miss Fiona is at the Willow cabin. We ran out of room here for all the donations."

"Ran out of room?"

Lucy shrugged. "The town is being very generous with their…stuff."

"You know what they say, Lucy. One man's trash is another man's treasure."

"I keep reminding myself of that."

"Here you go!" Poppy came into the room, her arms filled with a stuffed Snoopy almost as big as she was.

"There's more in the car." Carrying a large box, Dylan came in a few steps behind her.

"On the table there will be fine." Poppy pointed to the round kitchen table in the corner and looked over his shoulder. "I suppose we can bring the rest of it in here."

"Better take it straight to the Willow cabin. Your grandmother needs more space to sort and price."

"Is she doing that alone?" Poppy frowned.

"Your mom is helping. No services this weekend. Your sisters promised to come by later, and the Merry Widows are coming by tomorrow after church."

Dylan stretched his hand, gently setting it on her forearm. "Maybe we should go help?"

We? Harold bit back a smile.

"Good thing we dropped the puppy at Cindy's."

"Whoever adopts her is going to have to take a sibling as well or the poor girl may not be able to sleep at night." Dylan picked up the box again. "Which way are we going?"

There was that *we* again. Only a week and things were making progress. Nice progress.

• • • •

Sunshine streamed through the expanse of front windows at Hart House. Sunday was Poppy's favorite day of the week. She and her mom would have breakfast at the big house. Lucy always made enough food to put a five-star hotel brunch to shame. After church, the family would spend the day pretty much eating and decompressing. Not today.

"I swear." Lily slid her dish into the sink. "One of these Sundays they're going to have to wheel me out of here."

"I'm sure that's what half the town says after eating your desserts."

Lily sprouted a toothy grin. "Maybe."

"No maybe about it. It's easy to overindulge with any of the baked goods from the Pastry Stop."

"Okay ladies." Violet elbowed her way between the two sisters and placed her and her husband's dishes in the sink. "Somehow I'd forgotten how deliciously fattening Sundays are around here. I swore after breakfast that I would have a light lunch no matter what Lucy put in front of us."

"And then she slid that bowl of potato salad in front of you and—"

"All bets were off." Lily finished her sister Callie's sentence.

Violet shrugged. "I probably could have resisted the potato salad, and I knew I was in trouble with the glazed ham, but when she brought out the creamed corn—fresh creamed corn—it was a lost cause."

"Do you think she'll ever share that recipe with us?"

All heads in the room turned from side to side.

Lily sighed. "Like that joke on the internet, it's probably going to be engraved on the back of her headstone."

"What time is everyone heading for the balloon fest?" Heather carried in more dirty dishes.

Turning her wrist, Poppy looked at the time.

"Do you want to ride with us?"

It took Poppy a moment to register Heather had asked her a question.

"Or would you rather ride with Cole and me?" Lily smiled at her.

"Though it's only fair to warn you we're picking up Payton on the way and the man has a way of filling the backseat of anything smaller than a fire truck."

"Thanks, but that won't be necessary."

"Jake and I are riding with Cindy and Alan. Lucy asked us to take the woman in the Hickory cabin and make sure she wasn't left alone, but there's room for more people with that monster of an SUV."

Lily shook her head. "You'd better be careful. Lucy may have something up her sleeve for Payton and that woman."

"And if she does," Heather rolled her eyes, "you do not want to get caught in the crossfire."

Callie winced. "I wish you hadn't said that."

"So," Heather turned to her cousin, "you riding with us?"

Poppy shook her head. "I have a ride already."

"Who with?"

"Dylan."

"Dylan?" Lily froze at the sink and looked through the doorway toward the dining room where all the men were chatting like a coffee klatch of women. "You're going with Dylan?"

"Yes. I mean no." She shook her head. "I mean, not *with* with. Just…with."

Now her sisters and cousins were rooted to the floor, staring at her.

Some days she really needed to learn to keep her mouth shut. "I work with the guy." Sort of. "We promised Cindy we'd take the puppy around. Let it be known she's up for adoption along with three other siblings. That's it."

No one said a word and Poppy couldn't decide if they believed her, doubted her, or if she'd sprung a third eye on her forehead. The thing was, she wasn't sure if she believed her. Once she'd gotten over being furious with him for ruining her favorite hat, something about him had captured her attention like no other guy since her crush on her gym teacher in third grade. Looking back with adult perspective on a hotty factor, Dylan was definitely higher on the scale than Mr. Reidy. Especially since Dylan was kind and sensitive and thoughtful and Mr. Reidy, as nice as he was, paled in comparison.

A part of her screamed to steer clear. After all, his time here was temporary. Another part of her felt sure she'd be sorry if she didn't spend whatever time there was, however short, with this man. And of course, one very rambunctious puppy.

CHAPTER EIGHT

"This gal just does not wear out." Poppy reeled in the puppy's leash. "Ever."

She may have sounded a bit exasperated, but Poppy's grin belied her words. The chuckles, and smiles, and twinkling eyes told Dylan all he needed to know about this amazing woman. She was kind, thoughtful, and sensitive, and it wasn't an act. She clearly wasn't putting her best foot forward, she was just honest to goodness…nice. Any other job, any other place, and he'd be working seven days a week to get through, to see the final results, and then go home.

"I don't know." Dylan smiled back. Since Cindy couldn't handle three puppies at once, and she and Lucy had volunteered to help Katie with the One Stop's food booth, Dylan and Poppy agreed to take another one off her hands. "I think this one has even more energy."

A cuter, fluffier version of the pup they'd been caring for all week dragged him in every direction, constantly tangling him in the leash.

"You may be right. At the end of the day, they may be carrying us home."

"Now that you mention it." He laughed and tugged on the leash once again. "Unless these coats do the trick." The other thing Cindy had done was deliver the pups with coats that read *adopt me*. "Which way do we go?"

Poppy stuck her arm straight out. "That way. That's the food truck area. Let's see how Katie's doing."

"Ah. The way to a man's heart."

"Something like that." She laughed, slowing down at the sight of the line wrapped around Katie's spot.

"Another lobster roll," Katie called over to Lucy.

"Coming up, but at this rate we're going to run out of the mix."

"Run out?" Katie stood upright hands on her hips. "We've gone through four buckets?"

"Cleaned out of two," Cindy added. "Last one on deck."

"That's three." Katie narrowed her gaze at Cindy.

"Yes," Lucy said firmly. "Three buckets."

"Is there a problem?" Poppy asked, Dylan and the two pups beside her.

Katie shook her head. "Not really, just a missing bucket of lobster mix."

"Oh dear." Poppy seemed disproportionately concerned over a loss of a little food—even if it was Katie's lobster roll mix.

"Shall we check your car?" Dylan asked. He assumed the big white van parked behind them was hers.

Katie shook her head. "I was just in there to get more rolls. It's almost empty. If there'd been another bucket, I would have seen it."

Cindy finished assembling a corned beef sandwich and handed it off to the jilted Hart House guest that Lucy had roped into helping out with the customers.

"It must have been left at the One Stop." Katie's gaze focused into the distance. "I hate to leave you all here."

"I could go?" The guest looked up at Katie. "I'm the least busy of us."

"Do you know how to get there from here?"

"We could go," Poppy chimed in just as one of the puppies yanked at the leash unexpectedly, pulling her forward and tripping her over her own feet.

Katie let out a laugh. "You shouldn't be in such a hurry, little one." Turning, she faced Poppy. "You've got your hands full. Naomi can handle it."

Since Dylan knew all the names of everyone working the booth except the guest, he figured she must be Naomi.

Naomi untied her apron. "I'll hurry, I promise."

"Just stay safe." Lucy looked up from another sandwich.

"I'll be right back with the keys to the shop. Lucy, tell her where to find the fridge and about the handle." Katie turned on her heel.

"Can't miss the fridge. Go straight to the back, go behind the counter and you'll see the fridge on the left." Lucy's words trailed off as her gaze swung over to the parking lot, her eyes narrowing into thin slits. "Which car is yours?"

"The small red Ford."

"Thought so." Lucy shook her head. "You're blocked in by Brent's van." She stuck two fingers in the corners of her mouth and blew in the direction of the booth to her left. All heads snapped in her direction and she hollered at Brent. "You're going to have to move your van. Naomi here needs to get to the One Stop."

Brent nodded at Lucy, smiled at Naomi, and wiping his hands on a towel, hopped over the table. "Sure thing. Follow me."

"I need the—"

"Here are the keys. Thanks."

The two jogged to the parking lot and Dylan wondered what were the odds where he lived that so many neighbors and friends would come together to make something like this work.

Poppy turned to face him. "Why don't we come back after she's gotten more supply?"

He nodded. "Sounds good. Shall we check out the craft tent?"

"Sure." She flashed him a smile and tugging on the puppy's leash, moved forward at a brisk pace. Distracted by the scents surrounding the gondola of a large yellow balloon with primary colored dots, the puppy ground to a sudden halt. Almost tripping over the furball, Poppy's gaze lifted to the top. "No matter how many years I've come, these things always amaze me."

"I vaguely remember going to a balloon fest as a little boy. Watching all those balloons practice lift off yesterday morning was pretty cool. Made me feel a bit like a kid again." For the umpteenth time in the last half hour, Dylan extended the leash in an effort to both walk and untangle the puppy wrapped around him.

"Look." Poppy's free arm pointed upward and her grin lit up her face.

He cast his gaze to the sky and a bunch of small red, white, and blue helium filled balloons floated slowly into the air. "Those are used to determine if the wind speed and direction are fit for flying."

"I didn't know that, but it makes sense. I guess the wind is weak enough to let balloons fly this afternoon because it looks like the stars and stripes balloon is untethering."

"Sure does. And there's another one straightening up." Almost a football field away, another of the balloons that had been lying on its side was filling with air and tipping upright.

"How's it going?" Lily and her husband came to stop beside them. Each had a puppy on a leash.

"Oh my." The two new additions felt the need to pounce and play with their siblings, resulting in not two but four leashes tangling around Poppy's legs. Within seconds, one yanked left, the other pulled right and she was wobbling like a grazed bowling pin.

"Whoa!" Leaning forward, Dylan looped his arm around her waist and pulled her against him, struggling to stay upright on his own two feet. Who knew such small creatures could mess with a full grown adult male's sense of balance.

"Oh, no!" Lily lurched forward, dropping the one leash and almost tripped into the teetering couple.

Laughing out loud, Cole shook his head, planted his hands on either side of his wife's waist and pulled her upright. "Acrobats you guys will never make."

"Speak for yourself," Dylan deadpanned, looking about for the end of the leash. Any leash. He grabbed the one closest to him and almost knocked Poppy off her feet again and let it drop to the ground once more. "Sorry."

"Let's step back." Her hand on Dylan's shoulder for balance, Poppy lifted one leg up and out of the polyester loop, then shook her other foot out, slowly stepped back and teasingly squealed, "I'm free!"

"And so are they!" Easing his hands away from Poppy, ensuring she wasn't about to topple over, Dylan sprinted forward. In all the untangling, not one of the adults had managed to hang on to the end of a leash. Now, four puppies with a head start were in a full gallop across the field, and four screaming adults were chasing after them.

● ● ● ●

Poppy had never been more thankful she'd opted to wear loafers today and not her typical summer sandals. "How can such little things run so darn fast?"

"Low center of gravity, four legs." Dylan huffed beside her.

Even though she knew better than to take her eyes off the puppies, she lifted her gaze ahead and realized the lead puppy was heading straight for the steps in front of the stars and stripes balloon. The balloon preparing to fly. "Oh, no."

At her words, Dylan's gaze lifted into the distance and his brows pleated. "Oh, yes."

As if propelled by a magical force, he kicked into high gear and dashed ahead of Poppy. Sure enough, seconds before he caught up with the first pup, it launched itself up the stairs and flopped over and into the basket just as one of the men released another rope from the bumper it had been tied to.

Poppy heard him mumble, "Marvelous. Just marvelous," and then said a fast prayer that the dog and Dylan didn't wind up floating through the air for the next two hours.

"What the…" the guy by the stairs muttered loudly, his gaze suddenly meeting Dylan's as he rushed up the steps. "Hey, you can't—"

"Sorry, man. Just need a second." Dylan waved at the guy as he bolted up the stairs, into the basket, scooped up the trapped puppy, and hopped off again.

Outside the gondola, Lily, Poppy and Cole stood huffing, having successfully corralled the slower pups before the balloon company wound up with a litter in their basket.

"You were very naughty." Poppy shook her finger at the puppy in Dylan's arms. "Very naughty." Considering the way her tail wagged at a rapid clip, she doubted the dog had any idea she was being scolded.

His phone to his ear, Cole shook his head, disconnected the call and already backing up, handed his end of the leash to his wife. "I have to run. Our rig is the closest to the One Stop."

"The One Stop?" Lily's eyes widened with fear.

Cole shook his head, already trotting away, and called over his shoulder, "Two people are locked in the walk-in fridge."

Eyes fixed on Cole's back as he sprinted across the field to where his firefighter coworkers were already climbing onto the fire engine, Poppy and Lily shook their heads, then turned to face each other and echoed, "Lucy."

• • • •

"How in the name of all that is holy did those two wind up locked in the freezer?" Nadine Baker rearranged her cards. The day may have been longer and fuller than most, but there was always time for a late night card game at Hart House.

"Refrigerator, not freezer." Setting the remaining deck in the middle of the table, Ralph shook his head. "And the handle was loose. Didn't work from the inside anymore. Apparently, Katie thought Lucy was going to tell the woman not to let the door close all the way. She's probably kicking herself for not getting it fixed sooner."

Poppy peeked over the top of her cards at her partner. This afternoon had most definitely not been anything like she'd expected. Except for one thing. If she'd thought Dylan was special before, after watching him leap into a swaying gondola to save a puppy, she knew beyond any doubt this guy was definitely one of a kind. Her kind. Except he lived in Texas.

"And why didn't Katie tell the poor woman herself?" Louise, one of the merry widows, held her fanned out cards against her chest.

"She was otherwise occupied," Floyd answered. "Lucy said she got distracted by where the cars were parked."

"You can't blame a woman of my age for being a little forgetful." Lucy came in with a tray of fresh lemonades. "I noticed Naomi's car was blocked in and after we worked it out, I forgot to mention about the handle."

"An important thing to forget," the General said more softly than usual.

"At least," Lucy glared at the General, "there was no harm done."

"Other than being stuck in a cold refrigerator for almost an hour." Ralph closed his cards. "I bid three."

Poppy, Dylan, the General, and Thelma made up the second table.

"I hear you had a busy afternoon too?" the General asked Dylan. "I bid four."

"Pass." Dylan shifted his cards. "Nothing compared to being

locked in a refrigerator."

"But you saved a puppy from flying off into the wild blue yonder," Thelma added. "I mean, what if the poor thing had taken off and then jumped out?"

"I'm sure if we'd not caught her in time, someone in the gondola—"

"Gondola?" Louise called out.

Poppy looked up. "That's what they call the baskets under the hot air balloons."

"I'm sure someone would have kept the puppy safe. But I do think the puppy would have had a better time than the people in those cramped gondola things."

"How is your guest now?" Thelma asked.

"Staying in tonight," Grams answered. "Probably keeping warm under the covers with a good book."

As much as Poppy dreaded Lucy's antics, perhaps having been locked in close quarters anywhere today with Dylan wouldn't have been such a bad thing. Like it or not, she was falling a little too hard for this tall, dark Texan.

CHAPTER NINE

L iving in Texas, Dylan had heard a story or two of customers huddling into a walk-in refrigerator at a restaurant to seek shelter from a tornado. With the exception of that episode of the *Brady Bunch*, he couldn't remember ever hearing of someone locking themselves in a fridge by mistake.

"Of course, we understand," Poppy spoke into the handset of the church landline, and Dylan wondered if it had something to do with the puppy they'd dropped off at the Curl and Set this morning. With more foot traffic than the church, the owner had found a family for her puppy over the weekend, but maybe this poor gal was too energetic for such a busy place.

"It's okay. Really it is," Poppy continued. "I'll tell Pastor Bob."

Couldn't be the puppy if it involved the pastor. Dylan glanced at his watch and wondered if the apologies on the other end of the line might have to do with Brent not being here yet.

"Brent's tied up on an emergency job across the lake. Looks like we're going to have to wait a few more days to hang these paintings back up on the wall." Poppy pointed at the scattered frames leaning against the side wall of the office.

"How did those wind up back over there? Paintings shouldn't be exposed to direct sunlight." Lips pressed together, he shook his head and crossed the room. Just the other day he'd moved them away from the window. Nudging the stack away from the direct light, he paused at the Madonna in front. It was a stunning piece. Aside from the unexpectedness of this type of work, something about the painting stuck in his mind. Rather than simply push it out of the light like the others, he lifted the framed artwork for a closer look.

"It's beautiful, isn't it?" Poppy moved to stand slightly behind him. "It's one of my favorites in this room."

"It's Orthodox," he mumbled, distracted by the sweet scent of her perfume. Or maybe it was shampoo.

Her head tipped sideways, Poppy studied the painting almost as intently as he had been. Only now he was much more interested in the hint of green circling the edges of her brown eyes. How had he not noticed that before? Perhaps because until this very minute she'd not had reason to stand so close he could count the freckles on her nose.

"I'd never really thought about it. It's just beautiful."

"In western Christianity, Madonnas are usually more natural, more human. They tend to depict an average woman in an above average role. On the other hand, Orthodox artwork is always more celestial. Religious. The golden halo is typical."

"It's almost ironic."

"How so?"

"That a Jewish woman would donate an Orthodox Madonna to a small town church."

"Jewish?"

"Oh yes." Poppy turned and smiled up at him, her eyes dancing with delight. "She led a fascinating life. She and her sister escaped the Nazis by the hair of their chinny chin chin."

Chinny chin chin. He bit back a smile. From anyone else, the old-fashioned descriptor would have seemed out of place. From her it was rather endearing. Heartwarming.

"They were from Poland. Of course, things weren't going well for them under the Nazis and at some point a Christian friend had arranged travel to France, then England, with passage to the United States. The two families agreed that Mrs. Katz and her sister would join them, traveling as their own children, Becky and Debbie, to get them to safety. The hope was that some day their parents would join them."

"But that never happened?" So many stories of bravery and sacrifice came from that miserable time in history.

Poppy shook her head. "Mrs. Katz told me that her father had painted this for them. Told them to keep it with them and if they were separated from the Millers or questioned in any way, they were to casually show this as their prized possession painted by their papa."

"To support the illusion of two Christian children." It made sense. He'd heard stories of jewelers making crosses and Christian medallions for their children to wear in efforts to avoid the unthinkable.

"Didn't hurt that she and her sister were blue eyed blondes."

He nodded. "Fed into that mindset of a superior race."

"I'm afraid so. Long story short, the family made it to Boston. When the war ended and they learned the father and mother had not survived, the Millers raised the girls as their own. Mrs. Katz and her sister Debbie continued to champion programs for orphaned children all their lives. Debbie married and moved to California in the early sixties. I think she had one daughter. Mr. and Mrs. Katz never had children, unless you count all the children she helped."

"Sounds like you knew her well?" At this point, he was equally fascinated with the sparkle in Poppy's eyes as he'd been with the strokes of the Madonna. Maybe if there was time before he returned home to Texas, Poppy would let him paint her. *Home*. That thought gave him a physical pang of regret.

"Well enough. Mrs. Katz, or Becky as her friends called her, and her husband came up from Boston a few times in the summer and stayed at the cabins. She and my grandfather would talk for hours on the porch."

"I can see that."

"I loved listening to her stories. About life as a little girl, about leaving her father, about how he'd told her to never forget this painting was her treasure."

"Interesting." He hesitated to set it down where it might accidentally be damaged. "It's good, but I suspect he meant more a treasure of the heart."

She bobbed her head. "And Mrs. Katz did treasure it. That's why when she and her husband retired here at the mountain she decided to donate it to the church. Someplace it would be appreciated and more importantly, someplace as peaceful as Lawford Mountain. She didn't want it relegated to an attic and then destroyed."

"No. I can understand why it was important to her." From the smile on Poppy's face, he could see it was important to her as well. He loved how expressive her eyes were. And her smile. It was clear that she cared deeply for the people around her, both family and friends. He loved that about her too. His own words caught him by surprise. Love. Oh boy. There was most definitely something unique about this sweet brunette, and already he couldn't imagine working here without her. If he wasn't careful, Poppy Nelson was someone he could fall for. Hard. Or was it already too late?

• • • •

Poppy couldn't stop grinning. The memories of Mrs. Katz warmed her from the inside out, but having Dylan appreciate the old woman's gift to the church as much as she did held more importance than she'd expected. Even after she'd donated it to the church, Mrs. Katz had treasured the painting her father had given her, visiting regularly until the day she'd died. Now, Poppy treasured it because Mrs. Katz had loved it so.

"Isn't there someplace we could store these until Brent is finished in here?"

And there was the rub. So much was stored in the few closets they had, both the pastor and she feared that they'd be more likely to be damaged crammed behind a closed door than out in the open. "Not really. Unless…"

"Unless what?"

"The closet where we were keeping your shipments." She started out the door and down the hall, Dylan on her heels. "We didn't put too many things in there because we didn't know how much room you'd need for your supplies."

"It varies by job."

"With so much of your stuff in my office and the front hall…"

"There might be room for the paintings." It was the obvious thing for him to say. He wasn't actually reading her mind.

Coming to a halt in front of the large oak door, she wrapped her fingers around the knob and turned. Only nothing happened. Adding her second hand, she gave it another yank. Still nothing.

"Why don't you let me try?" Dylan inched so close that she could smell his cologne.

"Sometimes…" Or was it just his soap?

"Sometimes?" He stared down at her. Big brown eyes the color of rich caramel. "Poppy?"

She blinked. So lost in the depths of his gaze, she hadn't a clue what she was doing or saying or thinking.

"Sometimes…?" he coaxed.

"Yes." She really was going to have to make more effort not to stand so close. "Sometimes this time of year the wood swells and the door sticks a little. Since the fire it sticks more often."

"Got it." Large hands closed around the handle before she'd fully pulled her own away. "Sorry."

"No problem." She smiled and took a half step back just as he yanked at the door, frowned down at the handle and the wooden slab still firmly closed and with two hands, gave the door another tug. This time it flew open, almost knocking her off her feet.

There was nothing wrong with Dylan's reflexes. Before she even processed what had happened, his one hand rested firmly at her waist and the other on her shoulder, instantly holding her steady. "Whoa."

Her right hand shot out and latched onto his arm, her left landed flat on his chest. A rock-solid chest. If she thought they were standing too close a few moments ago, now she could feel his breath on her cheek and the rapid beat of his heart under her fingertips. *Don't look up.* But she did. Eyes a dreamy shade of caramel darkened to almost pitch black and drew her in like a magnet to true north. Her feet felt glued to the floor, and she couldn't have turned away even if another fire broke out.

"Poppy," his voice came out in a slow whisper as he leaned ever so slowly forward.

Her heart beat in double-time, her breath seemed to catch, and her eyelids drifted closed in anticipation of the sweet connection.

"Poppy," a deep, very male, very familiar voice rolled down the hall. Her grandfather.

"Yoo hoo," this time a decidedly female voice rang out.

Before she could react to the arrival of her grandparents, Dylan sucked in a deep breath and took a broad step in retreat. "I should go get the paintings."

All she could do was nod.

"There you are," Grams stated the obvious as Poppy moved away from the door—and Dylan. "I have wonderful news."

"You do?" Facing her grandmother, Poppy discreetly watched Dylan's back disappear up the hall.

"Yes. I just left Barbara at the Hilltop. She's moved a few things around so that we can have all the tables we need for the tag sale." Grams slapped her hands together enthusiastically. "Isn't that wonderful news? We won't have to worry about displaying all the donations that keep pouring in."

"No, we won't." Poppy did her best to give her grandmother a bright smile, but the near kiss with Dylan had left her rattled.

A painting in each hand, Dylan walked up to the closet door.

Pulling herself together, Poppy looked into the nearly empty closet. "I'll help with the rest."

"I can handle it. You can visit with your grandmother."

"No need. I said what I came to tell you." Grams pulled her into a quick hug with a kiss on each cheek and hurried off to where the General stood by the door, examining the work that had been completed over the last few days.

Following her grandmother as far as the office, Poppy thanked her grandparents for stopping by and hurried in to retrieve more paintings. What she needed right now was to keep busy, to keep her mind off the kiss that almost was.

CHAPTER TEN

"I can't believe how different it looks." Hat in hand and hooking her handbag over her shoulder, Poppy stood waiting for Dylan to finish cleaning up his tools for the day. Her gaze focused on the section of the mural that had been painstakingly cleaned, and he had to admit the delight in her eyes made him want to puff out his chest like a proud peacock. He might not be a master, but his work brought pleasure to people as much as the original artwork might. "Never ceases to amaze me what can be found after a hundred years of dirt and life have made themselves at home."

Poppy rocked back on her heels. "It must be really rewarding to bring a faded old piece back to its original glory. How did you ever find your way to this type of work?"

He wiped the last brush dry and set it on his work table. As his gaze cast downward at the last of the cleanup for the day, his mind jumped back in time, the astounding pictures playing in his head like an old movie reel. "I still remember the day my parents decided to take a family vacation to Italy. We had a tendency to follow Gramps when Uncle Sam sent him somewhere fun. He'd been in Hawaii for a couple of years when he got a special assignment that took him to the opposite end of the world. My mom insisted we follow. Of course, Gramps wasn't on vacation so the family did tours without him. Most of our time was spent in Rome and anything within a few hours drive. The Vatican was on the must see list. One last portion of restoration at the Sistine Chapel, the Last Judgment fresco, was underway. I got to see the before and after firsthand and it blew me away.

"My mother had a miserable time dragging me out of there. I managed to talk her into going back before we moved on to another part of the country. I suppose you could say I fell in love with the Sistine Chapel *and* restoration."

"Wow. Most people go to Italy and fall in love with a place."

"There is a lot to fall in love with in Italy. For some, it's Cinque Terre or Florence, for others it's the food, but for me it went just a little deeper. The art was everywhere, in all different forms. The massive carved doors on a cathedral, the bigger than life statue of a perfect David, the Birth of Venus by Boticelli, I could go on and on. All of it was amazing."

"Did you have a favorite?"

"Oh, yes. I remember the first time I stepped into the Cathedral in Bergamo. I couldn't stop staring at the ceiling. From every arch, to every inlay, to every angel, it was like staring at heaven. I'm surprised I didn't trip over anyone. Photographs don't do it justice. The camera can never capture the peace and tranquility that seeps into every pore when you're surrounded by so much artistry."

"I think I know what you mean. This two hundred year old church can't compete with a renaissance cathedral, but coming to work here every day, despite the frequent dysfunction of the board or some committee, always makes me forget the complications of the real world." A soft smile graced her lips. "For a long time Italy has also been someplace I've dreamed of traveling to, but now you make me want to go for a whole different reason."

His supplies cleaned and stored and ready for tomorrow, he came out from behind the table and had to shove his hands in his pockets. The urge to snatch her hand in his almost overwhelmed him. It felt as natural as breathing, and yet it seemed all wrong as well. Instead, he merely trudged forward, settling for briefly placing his hand along the small of her back as they maneuvered through the barrage of displaced items. "Bucket list item, huh?"

Poppy shrugged, falling into step beside him. "My mom and dad always wanted to go to Italy. Every year on New Years Eve they'd toast to next year in Italy."

"I gather they didn't make it?" From the far off look in her eye as she walked past him, placed her hat on her head, and proceeded out the church doors, he pretty much had his answer.

She didn't stop walking until they reached the car, then she turned to face him. "Daddy's death was unexpected."

"I'm so sorry for your loss." The words seemed to hold so little solace, but it was all he knew to say. Even for something that happened a long time ago. "I don't get to do very many restorations in Europe, but I've done a few. Maybe, I mean, if I go again, you could come too? I could show you the Italy I've learned to love."

A hint of pink tinged her cheeks. "I think I'd like that. Very much."

If he had buttons on his shirt they would have popped. People toss out someday promises all the time, but that she said yes so sweetly made him want very much to make this particular one come true.

She slid into the front seat. In silence she connected the seatbelt, reached for her throat as if intending to finger something that wasn't there, and blowing out a long sigh, her gaze lingered out the windshield a long moment before she turned to face him. "Some days having Daddy here doesn't seem all that long ago, and on other days it seems like he's been gone forever."

His own belt secured, he opened his mouth and in the nick of time remembered his grandfather's advice after his last breakup: sometimes women don't want you to fix it, they just want you to listen. So he nodded. "I can't imagine."

"Mom had such a hard time at first with the funeral home. She used to do the books but she wasn't really involved in the day to day stuff."

He'd actually forgotten that Virginia Nelson—a fiery redhead like her daughter Lily—ran a funeral parlor. The two images just didn't mesh. For whatever reason he more easily pictured the petite woman at the helm of a daycare or garden center. Funeral homes were for tall skinny men in black overcoats and tall hats. And wasn't that the most ridiculous cliché under the sun.

A hint of a smile tugged at one side of her mouth. "Daddy had a way of making the most *not* normal situation seem perfectly normal. Once, and I shouldn't laugh because it really isn't funny, but if a casket is flawed from the factory, you really won't know until funeral day."

"Uh oh."

Her smile grew. "Yep. Penelope Dunkirk had a lot of money and never missed a chance to let a person know it. Don't get me wrong, she donated it generously, but everything always had to be exactly her way."

"As in the Dunkirk library?"

Poppy nodded. "That was the only way to get the money for the updated children's wing."

"Got it."

"So, she had a rather formal funeral. A hardwood, metal-plated casket that was absolutely beautiful—and heavy."

He resisted the urge to grimace.

"The gurney couldn't be used up the steps of the church so the pallbearers held onto the sides and slowly inched their way up and into the church foyer. They were about to slide the gurney under once again when the bottom of the casket fell away. It—*and* Mrs. Dunkirk—slid into the church like a toboggan down the driveway."

"Oh no."

"Oh yes. One huge gasp filled the church. Mom always sat in one of the back pews and I don't think I've ever seen her face such a ghostly shade of white. Looking back, I'm surprised she didn't pass out."

"Daddy calmly walked around the casket, faced the congregation and said, *Penelope always did love to make a big entrance.* The whole church cracked up, and Daddy and the pallbearers quickly set everything in place on the gurney. Then between the funeral and the graveside service the bottom was firmly, and permanently, reattached. Thank heavens Mom has never had to deal with something like that on her own."

"He sounds like quite the guy."

A glint of sadness returned to her eyes.

He couldn't stand to see her not happy. "What do you say if we break with routine?"

A flicker of interest sparked in her gaze. "What were you thinking?"

That he had about ten minutes to figure out where was the highest public access to the mountain, where was the best place to get a bottle of wine, and pray this wasn't the dumbest idea he'd ever had.

• • • •

Poppy had no idea what had come over her talking about her dad and growing up in a funeral parlor family. She and her sisters and mom would talk about him or about how things were always just a little different for them, especially when you're ten years old and wanted to have a slumber party but no one liked the idea of sleeping at the undertaker's house. Even if their lakeside home had never had a dead body in it. At least not that they knew of. But she never really talked about her dad anymore, especially not to someone she'd only known for a little over a week.

"Who knew the best place to buy wine is the same place to buy bait for fishing, gas for boating, and lobster rolls for lunch," Dylan said as he pulled into the One Stop parking lot.

"We have a liquor store in town, but if you want cheese and crackers too, there's no reason to make two stops."

"Agreed." He trotted around the front of the car in time to open her door for her.

She really loved that about him. Most of the guys she'd dated had hung on to the small courtesies that helped make a woman feel special, but a few too many had no trouble treating her like just one of the guys.

"Well now." Katie looked over her shoulder from a shelf she'd been stocking. "Isn't this a nice surprise? Is Lucy needing some more soda bread? I have one loaf left."

"Not today." Poppy grinned at the favorite shopkeeper, but the smile that bloomed from deep inside probably had more to do with her growing affection for the man now scanning the shelves than her love for Katie.

Wiping her hands on the small apron she wore, Katie turned to face them. "Then what might you be having?"

"One bottle of Pinot Noir, if you have it," Dylan continued searching the shelves as he spoke.

Katie pointed to the wine corner. "We do."

"Some cheese. Maybe a brie and—"

"Ooh!" Katie almost squealed with delight. "An evening picnic. I have a wonderful camembert, or better yet, port wine Vermont cheddar." She paused to look at Poppy then back to Dylan. "Just the two of you?"

They both nodded and Katie's already wide grin grew impossibly brighter. "Then you'll want my last baguette. Perfect crunch for a good brie." Within moments she'd piled plastic plates, silverware, napkins, wine, cheeses, bread, grapes and lastly… "Try this. A little country sausage. Not quite like they make in France, but close."

"Thank you." Dylan flashed an appreciative smile. "That will be perfect."

"Heading out onto the lake? It's going to be a starry night."

"Actually," he shifted his weight, "I was thinking of someplace up high. Closer to those stars."

Katie stopped, looked from one to the other. "If you don't mind a suggestion, tonight would be an especially good night for a picnic on the water. I have it from a reliable source that floating in the middle of the lake is the only way to avoid, ehm, shall we say interruptions."

"Thank you, but—" Poppy's phone chimed in her pocket. Turning her back to everyone, she held up a finger and whispered excuse me. "Hello?"

"Oh good. Haven't been able to get any of your sisters or cousins to answer their phones."

Alarm shot through Poppy from her toes to her hairline at the General's words. "Is something wrong?" Her brain scrambled through all the possibilities. Her grandmother, Lucy, her mother.

"Not the way you think."

What other way is there? She didn't voice the question, but the frown on her face must have shown her thoughts because Dylan stepped into her space, gently resting his hand on her shoulder. The sweet comfort of the gesture was enough to scramble her brain for completely different reasons than a moment ago.

"Can you help?" the General asked.

What? Oh crud. She really was too easily distracted around this man. "I'm sorry, sir. What did you say?"

"The boat. Can you take the boat?"

"Boat?"

"Young lady, do you have cotton in your ears?"

"I'm sorry. I'm at the One Stop and didn't hear all you said." That was the truth. She simply neglected to mention the reason she didn't hear had more to do with the hand on her shoulder than the four walls surrounding her.

"The guests in the Sycamore cabin checked out and we offered to return the boat rental to the marina for them."

Poppy nodded at the phone. That was a service her grandfather often offered.

"Well, it turns out that Bobby needs it back at the marina to do whatever he does before handing it over to the reservation for tomorrow morning and he can't break loose right now. Your grandmother and Lucy are in town at the Ladies Art League meeting and we're expecting new guests from Texas. Someone has to stay here."

"Oh, uh." Her gaze shifted to Dylan and the food already neatly packed and ready to go. "I, uh…"

Dylan nodded. She wasn't sure if he heard her grandfather's end of the conversation or not, but it was clear that no matter what, he like her put family first. Lord, didn't that make her love him even more. *Love* him?

"Are you still there?" the General's voice boomed.

"Yes, sir. Sorry, sir. We'll be at Hart House shortly."

"Is it serious?" Dylan asked quickly.

"Nothing for us to be a worrying now, is there?" Katie slid the picnic snacks across the counter. "Your grandmother and grandfather look so good for their ages. It's hard to think they may not be as young and independent as they once were."

"I'm not sure I'm convinced they'll ever need anyone's help."

"So it's all good?" Dylan asked.

"Well, that depends on whether or not you consider taking a guest's boat back to the marina tonight a good or bad thing."

"As long as I get to come along with you, anywhere is good." With a cute lopsided grin, he scooped up his purchase, waved at Katie, and moved to hold the exit door open for her.

Yep. She definitely could get used to this. Too bad she wasn't likely to get the chance.

CHAPTER ELEVEN

Sometimes life just worked out and tonight was most definitely one of those nights.

"I really appreciate this." The General tipped the laptop lid closed and pushed to his feet. "Your grandmother and Lucy should be home any minute. Meg and her husband should be arriving in about an hour or so. They'll be joining us for dinner so we might have to eat a bit later than usual."

"Oh." Poppy's eyebrows lifted slightly.

"I'm sure they're going to be tired. This is a long trek for them."

"Good friends?"

Her grandfather paused and smiled. "I'd like to think so. They own a bed and breakfast in West Texas. We met through the family innkeeper group."

Dylan watched Poppy's gaze follow her grandfather's movements.

The older man glanced around his impeccably kept office and continued into the main hall where he tugged a set of keys from a hook behind a massive antique desk. "Here are the keys for the boat. There will be extra time till dinner if you two want to take a little ride around the lake. It's a lovely evening."

"I thought Bobby was in a hurry to get the boat back to the marina?"

"Well, he needs an hour with the boat. The marina doesn't close till nine." The General reached for another key with a bright yellow pom pom. "I think I'll double-check the cabin. Make sure all is ship shape. Excuse me."

With that, the General marched out the front door and down the path.

"Shall we?" Dylan extended an elbow. "Wonder how hard it is to eat cheese and crackers on a moving boat."

"Not hard at all."

His steps slowed. "You've had a lot of experience with this, have you?"

Flattening her hand atop her hat, she tipped her head back and that sweet laugh spilled forth. "Anyone who's grown up on a lake can practically walk on water." Her hand stretched out to his. "Come on."

"Oh, this I have to see." Picnic goodies in one hand, his other hand latched onto her dangling fingers and followed her down the stone steps, along the path, past the cabins with colorful doors, past what he knew was her cabin, his mind drawing pictures of what her home might be like. By the time they reached the end of the Point where the sports boat was docked, his imagination had created an entire world in living color of how Poppy spent her downtime, and he liked every bit of it.

Even though he could count on one hand the amount of times he'd been on a small boat, and considering how little time he'd spent with Poppy away from the confines of the church restoration project, the two maneuvered their way into the boat, handing off the food and drink as easily as any couple who'd spent years of free time together. He truly loved that not a single awkward moment passed between them.

"I hope you don't mind too much that we had to adjust your plans?" Poppy looked around the small cruiser.

"Not at all. This may be a step up from what I had in mind."

"Really?"

He waved at the small table and seating area bolted to one side. "This looks way more comfortable than a blanket on the hard ground."

"Agreed." She smiled, carefully removing her hat and placing it under the seat storage. This wasn't the first time he'd seen her wearing the hat he'd bought her. At the time he'd hoped she might enjoy it as much as she had the one he'd accidentally ruined. Now he hoped he'd be around long enough to see her wear it again and again.

"So, Captain, what do you say if we get started and find a quiet spot along the way to drop anchor, enjoy a little nosh, and then deliver the boat?" Already he could see how her mood had lifted from earlier in the day. He really did like the twinkle in her eyes when she smiled from the heart. Standing beside her, his fingers itched to rest at her back or on her shoulder. Instead he shoved them in his pockets and kept his gaze on the horizon. This really was an amazing place.

"How about there?" Poppy slowed and pointed to a cove to the right.

The carved out spot along the edge of the lake looked like it belonged in a watercolor from the turn of the last century. Willow trees dotted the landscape and the kaleidoscope of shades of green painted a stunning picture. "That looks perfect."

"It's the General's favorite fishing spot. Actually, probably Rose's too."

"She fishes?"

"No, but she did sort of hook Logan there."

"Sort of?"

"Well," Poppy blushed, "she'd actually been learning how to cast when the only thing she'd caught all day was Logan."

It took Dylan a few minutes to determine she wasn't kidding and most likely meant exactly what she'd said. "As in rod and reel?"

"Hook, line and sinker." The pink in her cheek brightened. "Sorry, couldn't resist."

"Well, it is a unique way to meet a man."

"About as unique as hitting him with your car in the middle of the road."

Surely she had to be kidding this time. "Who did that?"

"Lily. On her way to work in the morning she hit Cole while he was jogging."

"Clearly, since I've met them both, everything turned out fine."

"As long as Lucy didn't burn the house down."

"I don't think I want to know." He bit back a laugh. "Do I?"

"Probably not." Her nose scrunched in a cute grin. "Of course, Cindy thought Alan was a serial killer."

"Okay, now you have to be pulling my leg."

"No. She met him over a stray wild animal, found what she thought was a hostage tied to a chair, and later found him stabbing at a rib roast like Norman Bates in *Psycho*."

"You're not kidding?" Maybe this family wasn't as Rockwellian as he'd thought. "Wait. Isn't Cindy married to the famous mystery writer?"

Tapping the tip of her nose with her pointer finger, Poppy's grin spread from ear to ear. "Apparently he acts out quite a bit of his plots."

That made Dylan laugh. He could just imagine how gruesome a scenario Cindy might have stumbled into. "I'll keep that in mind."

The boat slowed as Poppy steered it into the picturesque cove. "I'll drop the anchor."

"I never realized how peaceful the sounds of water lapping against a boat are."

Poppy glanced over her shoulder, her grin infectious. "Everything about this lake is peaceful."

"Duly noted."

"If you'll take the helm a minute." She stared at him for a brief moment before giggling. "The steering wheel."

"Ah. What do you want me to do?" He took over the wheel while she stepped away.

"Just keep her steady for a moment while I check on something. Then we should have about thirty minutes or so to enjoy our appetizers before Bobby misses us at the marina and the General's special guests arrive."

"Just enough time for a nice glass of wine and what Katie promises to be very good cheese."

"And ready," she said softly.

Still holding onto the large wheel, he turned, surprised to find her back and standing up close.

Her fingers rested on his. "You can let go now."

At that moment, she shifted her attention from his hands to his face and as if only now realizing just how close they were standing, her eyes widened, her lower lip dropped slightly open, and he quickly calculated that if he tipped his head just so…

• • • •

Poppy didn't know how she'd miscalculated her position. She hadn't meant to stand so close. To invade his personal space. Or had she? All she knew was she'd looked up and saw fire in his big brown eyes and lost her breath. Another second and his head tipped forward and all coherent thought slipped away. Had anyone ever kissed her with such tenderness, such care?

Gently, he pulled back and not till the cool evening breeze touched her lips did she realize that strong fingers tenderly held her waist.

"That was nice."

It took an extra beat for her to register the words. Somehow the heat of his hands seemed to be short-circuiting the connectors between her brain and her mouth. No words were forthcoming.

A deep line creased his forehead and his hands quickly dropped to his sides. "I'm sorry if I—"

"No." She snatched his retreating hand in hers and swallowing hard, squeezed his hand. "I mean, yes. It was very nice."

His frown slipped and a hint of a smile tugged at the corners of his mouth until his eyes twinkled with merriment, or perhaps mischief. "Want to do it again?"

"What about the wine?" she teased. "And cheese?"

Looping his arm around her middle, he tugged her a fraction closer, lowered his head until he was only a breath away, and whispered against her lips, "You're all I need."

She was definitely going to have to thank her grandfather for setting the church on fire. Later.

• • • •

"Thanks for bringing her in." Bobby greeted them at the dock. With his help, it didn't take long to tie the boat up. "Perfect timing. I just finished up another boat heading out tomorrow morning. While I get started on this, my brother is doing a dinner run. He can drop you off at Hart House."

"That'll be great. Thanks." Poppy wondered why if the brother had time to take them home, he didn't have time to pick up the boat himself, but she was happy to have spent a precious few minutes enjoying the only real privacy she and Dylan had had since his arrival. If she had anything to say about it, she was going to do her level best to find some more stolen long minutes.

They'd made it halfway across the parking lot when Bobby

called out to them, holding up the untouched bottle of wine. "Looks like you forgot something."

Her cheeks flushed and she glanced up at Dylan. The man showed no such signs of embarrassment. Not that they'd done anything warranting embarrassment, but somehow making out with a guy she hadn't known that long while tucked away in a hidden cove made her feel just a little bit risqué. It was silly, but she couldn't help it.

The wine in one hand and the bag of cheese and baguette in the other, Bobby hurried toward them.

Dylan raised his hand and shook his head. "Keep it. Take your best girl out for a moonlight ride."

Stopping in his tracks, Bobby looked at the wine then back to Dylan. "You sure? This is good stuff."

He looked at her. "Should we take it back to the house?"

"I'd rather not explain why we never got around to opening the bottle."

"That's what I thought." He lifted his chin toward the marina manager. "We're sure. Enjoy."

And just like that they were riding across town, pulling onto the main Hart property, and walking onto the porch and a flurry of activity.

"Dylan?" a deep voice questioned.

"Adam." A bright smile greeted the man. "What the heck are you doing here?"

Adam's gaze dropped to Poppy, their eyes briefly met and the handsome man smiled. "Probably the same thing you are."

"Dylan." A lovely redhead sidled up beside the man Dylan called Adam. "This is certainly a surprise."

"I see you know our resident restoration expert." The General came up behind the two guests from Texas.

Dylan nodded. "I first met Meg years ago when she interviewed me to restore a couple of pieces for a boutique hotel in Dallas." Quick introductions were made for Poppy's benefit.

"It really is a small world, isn't it?" Fiona Hart smiled, leaning in beside her husband.

"It gets even smaller every day," Adam interjected with a smile.

"And why," hands tightly gripping a tray laden with fresh lemonades, Lucy shook her head, "is everyone gathering in the front hall like a gaggle of confused geese? This tray isn't getting any lighter."

Instantly everyone scurried in Lucy's direction to render aid. With each person taking a glass, whether they were thirsty or not, the tray quickly emptied.

Lucy turned toward the kitchen and called over her shoulder, "Dinner will be ready soon. Go ahead and take a seat on the porch. Pretty soon it's going to be too cold to sit outside."

Like good soldiers following orders, everyone practically marched outside. Seated in one of the many green rockers and looking at the glass in her hand, Meg was the first to take a sip. "Oh, my. This is delicious."

"Who knew lemonade could taste so good?" Adam chimed in, taking another long gulp. "It gets awfully hot in west Texas in the summer months."

"I was just thinking the same thing." Meg met her husband's gaze.

Poppy was pretty sure the two were having a long conversation despite remaining perfectly silent. She didn't really remember if her parents had ever done that, but she'd certainly seen her grandparents do it with some regularity. Reaching from one chair to another, their hands met and linking fingers, the two smiled with a slight nod. An agreement had clearly been made.

"I wonder." Without letting go of her husband's fingers, Meg turned to the General. "What do you think are the odds Lucy will share her recipe?"

"Quite good, I'm sure," the General answered. "After all, that's why you're here. To discover what we can learn from each other."

"That's very kind of you," Meg responded. "But considering that your family has been innkeeping for generations, I expect to be doing all the learning."

"Nonsense. There's always room to learn something new." Pushing off with her toe, Grams set the rocker in motion and breathed out a small sigh.

For the first time in ages, Poppy realized her grandmother wasn't involved with a new hobby. As a matter of fact, it had been at least a week or longer since Grams had last worked on a project. What was that all about?

"You okay?"

It took a moment to register that the soft voice nearly whispering in her ear was Dylan leaning into her, concern painted clearly on his face. "Sorry," she whispered back. "Just distracted."

His chin dipped in understanding, but his gaze held a strong streak of concern. Or possibly doubt.

"Really," she reassured him with her best effort at a smile.

Not looking completely convinced, he seemed to finally let go of his concern.

"I know it's the same sky as West Texas, but with all the tall trees and mountains, the view is surprisingly different." Her head leaned back in the high back seat, Meg focused on the distant sky. "I bet the lake is amazing during a full moon."

One by one, her cousins and sisters came up the steps. The buzz of conversation grew loud enough that they could probably be heard across the mountain, but that didn't matter, Poppy loved having a big noisy family. She could see Dylan looking at Lily and Cindy with fresh eyes. She almost laughed out loud when he tilted his head to one side and studied Alan, Cindy's author husband, rolling a long-handled teaspoon in his hand. Good thing he wasn't playing with knives. Poppy found herself wishing she could lean over and kiss Dylan again.

"Dinner's on," Lucy announced and the family paraded across the hall and into the dining room. Discussion carried on, everything from antique decorations, to inn friendly recipes, to the best way to bribe a little kid without them knowing what you were doing. A little later and they were back on the porch, fittingly fed and watered and not surprisingly, their sweet tooth more than satisfied.

"I have to give my wife credit where credit is due." Adam held a beer bottle in his hand and kept his gaze out the window to the moon playing hide and seek on the lake. "Same starry sky for the most part, yet this one looks so different."

Poppy refrained from holding Dylan's hand the way so many of her family was doing with their significant others, but she couldn't really keep her eyes off of him. She'd look at who ever was talking, interject a word or two, but mostly her gaze kept darting back to the man squinting at the distant moonlight. She'd pay big bucks to know what he was thinking.

Another swath of billowy clouds passed in front of the bright moon, sending the lakeside cabins into slight darkness until the brisk wind blew them out of the way.

"Even the clouds formations are different." Meg continued to stare up at the sky. "I mean," she laughed, "oh,I don't know what I mean anymore."

Dylan's gaze focused, his eyes snapped from narrow slits to wide-eyed wonder. "Good heavens. I think I've got it."

"Got what?" Poppy tried to figure out what he was looking at.

"What's been bothering me." He snatched hold of her free hand. "If I'm right, tomorrow isn't going to come soon enough."

CHAPTER TWELVE

Morning couldn't come fast enough for Dylan. He hadn't wanted to blurt out his suspicions, in case he was completely off base. If he was right, the possibilities were exhilarating. Taking a few moments to divert the conversation away from his rushed declaration, but by breakfast it hadn't made much of a difference. He had pretty much let everyone at the table in on his thoughts and now like a parade, an entourage of friends and guests followed him into Poppy's office.

"Which painting?" The General's gaze darted around the vestibule.

Poppy led the way down the nearest hall. "In the storage closet."

"This is really quite exciting, isn't it?" Fiona Hart rubbed her hands together and grinning like a schoolgirl, followed her husband.

"I admit, this is rather fun." Meg, who had eagerly listened in on the conversation over breakfast, held on tightly to her husband's hand and followed close behind Mrs. Hart.

"Here we go." Poppy stopped at the door and took a deep breath. Hand on the knob, she slowly turned the hardware and swung the door open.

"I still can't believe you figured this out from a full moon and a cloud." Mrs. Hart peered over her granddaughter's shoulder.

"Something about the painting had been bothering me almost since I first saw it. Orthodox paintings have deep colors but this one seemed so dark. Even when the sunlight was shining against it. Or rather behind it."

"Still an excellent observation," the General confirmed.

"Careful," Mrs. Hart urged Poppy as she backed out of the small storage space. "Oh. It is pretty. I've always liked that painting. So different from the others on display."

"Yes," Poppy agreed.

"I see what you mean." Now Meg Farraday stared, eyes

narrowed, at the painting.

Gingerly, Poppy handed it over to him and he carried it back to her office. The entourage following him in a single file line. Silence hung heavy as he removed the canvas from the frame. More than once in his career he uncovered paintings over a painting, but never with an audience watching his every move so intensely.

He examined the front, the strokes, and the colors carefully, before flipping it to do so from behind. "I wish I had access to some of my dating tools for testing the paint and canvas."

"Would any art museum have access to that equipment?" the General asked.

He nodded. "Some. If they're large enough."

"But," Poppy added, "if they don't have it themselves, surely they must have access to it?"

"Definitely," he confirmed.

"And problem solved." Poppy pulled out her phone. "I'll call Rose."

That was right. He'd forgotten that one of the granddaughters was the curator for a large museum in Boston. Something still didn't feel right. He turned the canvas once and again.

"What's wrong?" Poppy asked. "What are you thinking?"

Was it absolutely ridiculous that it made him want to smile thinking she knew him well enough in this short time to recognize something didn't sit right with him? "Even for a painting on a painting, it feels a little heavy." He moved over to his toolbox and pulled out something to tinker with the tacking on the back of the frame.

"You have something in mind?" Meg inched a little closer to him.

"Maybe. Probably a crazy idea." Running his fingers over the back edge of the canvas, he felt sure he was on the right track. Gently easing out one of the tacks, he picked at the edge and felt his cheeks tag at the corners of his mouth. "Bingo."

"What?" Poppy moved close enough to be pressing against him.

"I think what we have is two canvases."

All eyes were on the back of the painting as he one by one lifted each tack.

"Holy cow." Poppy's hand lifted to her mouth as the backing of the original canvas was exposed.

"I wonder what it could be?" Mrs. Hart took a step closer, her gaze remaining on the painting.

Adam spoke for the first time. "We're going to find out soon enough."

"It could be nothing." But Dylan's gut told him it was something or it would have been painted over, not covered up.

Poppy glanced at him without fully turning her head. He could read in her eyes that she knew his words did not represent what he was actually thinking. So now she knew him, and he knew her. Everything about them, this place, and this situation with the painting, was simply extraordinary—and delightful. And wasn't that an odd feeling. Delightful.

"Did you find something wrong?" The General, like everyone else in the room, was riveted to Dylan's fingers working the painting without reading his face.

And a good thing too. Otherwise they might have noticed nothing was wrong with the painting, he was merely distracted by thoughts of his relationship—if you could call it that—with Poppy when he should be focusing on what could be a fantastic discovery. Or flop. "No. Just being careful."

Having removed all the tacks, he tested one corner. The second canvas easily slid away from the original. Not till the two separated without issue did he realize the level of his apprehension that removing the top canvas after decades and generations of being pressed together might damage the painting beneath it.

"This is more exciting than watching the Powerball numbers," Mrs. Hart exclaimed as he peeled away the Madonna.

The woman had a good point. Odds were very likely the painting underneath would have little more import than the visible Madonna, but like with the lottery, hopes were high that it could be the winning ticket for the church.

This was it. Sucking in a deep breath, he flipped the painting over to see what lie beneath. A collective gasp filled the room.

"Good lord," Meg muttered softly. "Is that what I think it is?"

Dylan stared, stunned. "Depends on whether or not you're

thinking what I'm thinking."

"I'm thinking that's a Degas."

Heaven help him, that's what he was thinking too.

• • • •

Poppy didn't know a whole lot about art, but he she knew a line of ballerinas was most definitely in the style of Degas. "Now what?"

"Good question." Unmoving, Dylan stared at the painting.

"Wow," Adam mumbled.

"Yes," the General added. "If this is what we all seem to think it is, the storage closet doesn't seem like a terribly appropriate place for a painting potentially worth millions."

"Probably not, but this could merely be a good copy by the same person who painted the Madonna." Dylan's mouth was the only thing moving. His gaze remained riveted to the painting.

"But you don't think so, do you?" Poppy asked.

He blew out a long, slow breath. "I'm not an appraiser, but the layering looks good, the brush strokes. I'd have to research the signature, but if this is what I think it is, this could be any number of his works that have been missing since the war."

"So where do we start?" she almost whispered. Just being in the same room with a painting that might be a masterpiece filled the air with a sense of awe she'd never experienced before.

"Rose," the General answered.

Dylan nodded. "It needs to be authenticated."

"And traced," Adam said more sternly. "I hate to be the bearer of bad news, but if this is indeed a Degas, it may very well be one of the many looted paintings taken by the Nazis."

"Which means it may not have been Mrs. Katz's to give if it belonged to someone else," Poppy finished.

"Exactly." Adam nodded.

"So we'd best do some research on missing Degas." The General took a step back.

"What's Rose's number?" Dylan asked.

"I'll call her." The General pulled out his phone.

Poppy reached for her own phone. "I'll call Kathleen Regatta.

Besides being one of Zinnia's dearest friends and having spent as much summer time as any of us on the lake, she's a top notch reporter. Maybe with the donor's name she can help track down the history of this painting."

"Good idea," the General agreed. "She'll probably need Rebecca's father's name. He's the one who seemed to know he'd given his daughter a treasure."

"Oh, that's right," Poppy snapped her fingers. "Katz was her married name. Miller was the name she was brought up with, but I don't believe I know her father's name. Well, uncovering his name should hopefully be right up Kat's alley."

"Who's going to tell Pastor Bob?" Grams asked.

"Oh." Poppy disconnected the call. Since the painting, or at least one of them, belonged to the church, she didn't technically have the right to go calling a whole lot of people about this without discussing it first with the pastor, and probably the board. The pastor wasn't so bad, but as well as she knew her own name, she knew the board was only going to muck it up. As her grandmother often said, it was easier to ask forgiveness than permission. She made an executive decision. "I'll speak with Kat, then call the pastor."

"That won't be necessary." Dylan waved a finger toward the window. "Pastor just pulled in."

Then she'd better talk fast.

• • • •

"When will we know if the painting is trash or treasure?" Lucy had many gifts, especially in the kitchen, but diplomacy was not one of them.

"Rose is driving up tomorrow. She's bringing someone on the QT with her. They'll do an initial evaluation." Poppy couldn't believe how fast everything was moving. Since telling the pastor of their possible find, phones had been going off left and right, and it was all they could do to keep the whole town from knowing. Though she was pretty sure that like it or not, by tomorrow the whole mountain would probably know there was a potential masterpiece in the church's collection.

"You do realize if this is an original Degas," Lily pulled a stack of silverware from the drawer, "the church's financial woes will disappear."

"A lot of good could be done with that kind of money." Callie reached for a stuffed mushroom at the same time as Poppy. "Hey, you've already had half the tray. This one has my name on it."

"Sorry." Pulling her hand back, she smiled contritely at her sister. She couldn't help it if she had a healthy appetite and a strong metabolism to match. Especially when she was nervous. The urge to graze non-stop always settled in. Between her conversation with her longtime friend who promised to do the best she could even if stolen Nazi art wasn't quite the same is digging up the dirt on a mafia connected socialite, determining where to store the potentially priceless artwork before the whole town learned of its existence, and one by one talking each of the board members down from the rafters at the good news that no one was totally sure of, Poppy's urge to eat her way into oblivion had kicked in full force.

"Here, dear." Lucy slid a dish of her famed bacon-wrapped stuffed dates under Poppy's nose. Bless her.

"Those look good." Dylan inched closer, sniffing the air.

Poppy lifted the plate in his direction as an offering. "That's because they are."

"Thanks." His eyes sparkled, and her heart did a tap dance.

The sound of a barking puppy and scurrying paws against hardwood reached the kitchen moments before Poppy's charge of the other day came barreling into the room and bounced around her ankles. Dutifully at their master's sides, Sarge and Lady ignored the bouncing ball of fluff.

"That puppy has more energy than any puppy I've ever known." Cindy came through the doorway, dropped her bag on a bench and headed straight for the stuffed dates. "What broke now?"

"Broke?" Lucy closed the oven door and spun to face Cindy. "You mean something happened to the painting?"

"Painting? What painting?" Her gaze on the puppy now dancing around Dylan's feet, Cindy popped the date into her mouth.

The whole room stopped and stared at the eldest Nelson daughter.

"The Degas." Lily looked at her older sister as though she'd sprouted a date tree on her head.

Cindy's hand froze midway to her mouth with another date. "The what?"

"Wait." Poppy waved her hands. "What do you mean what broke?"

"Brent's truck is parked in front of the Hickory cabin." The puppy at her feet now, Cindy bent down to scratch her ears. "What Degas?"

"Our Brent? Carpentry Brent?" Lucy hurried to the back door and looked through the glass in the direction of the Hickory cabin.

"Really?" Lily leaned over Lucy's shoulder. "I didn't know something was broken."

"It's not." Lucy continued to stare out the windowed door. She suddenly spun to face the General. "Is it?"

The older man shook his head.

"Who cares about the Hickory cabin." Standing upright, Cindy almost stomped her feet. "What's this about a Degas?"

"How many people know about this?" Rose came walking through the door, a tall man with graying temples behind her.

"What are you doing here?" Lucy asked.

"Nice to see you too." Rose smiled at the woman, then turned more seriously to her cousin. "Does the whole town know yet?"

Poppy scooped the still dancing puppy into her arms. "I hope not, and I thought you weren't coming until tomorrow?"

"You tell me you may have found a missing Degas and are surprised I moved heaven and earth to get here as fast as I could?" Rose turned to the man beside her. "This is Ed Wagner, best art appraiser in the business, and lucky for me, a Degas expert. He was kind enough to drop everything and come up from Manhattan." She waved an arm from one end of the kitchen to the other. "This is my family."

Each person waved and said their name. With a family so big, they'd nailed down the simplest way to do large gathering introductions ages ago.

"So." Rose straightened her shoulders and rubbed her hands together. "When can we hit the church and take a look?"

"That won't be necessary." The General shook his head.

Rose's forehead crinkled like a ridged potato chip. "What do you mean?"

"I mean, it's not there anymore."

If there was a facial expression for complete horror, Rose's face wore it.

The General raised his hands, palm out. "Don't get your bloomers in a twist. We moved it to some place more secure."

"And that would be?"

"My office. It's in my gun safe."

"Never thought there'd be a good reason for such a big safe until now," Grams teased. The woman never did care much for guns but accepted it was a part of her husband's job.

Poppy wasn't sure whose face beamed more brightly, Rose's or the expert's.

"Shall we?" Rose gestured toward the door.

Lucy put her hands on her hips. "What about supper? It will be ready any minute."

Jaw open slightly, Rose turned doe-eyed at Lucy.

The family housekeeper shook her head. "Never mind. Forget I said that. I'll keep dinner warm. Take your time."

"Thanks."

The expert and Dylan walked side by side, Rose only a step ahead of them. Words like patina and pine were batted back and forth in the conversation and Poppy got the impression that Dylan was much more certain of his findings than he'd let on. The two men continued talking as the General unlocked his safe and Rose carefully pulled out the canvas in question. The room grew very quiet as Ed took a step forward, looked at it, turned to Rose, and then removing a magnifying glass from his pocket, leaned over the corner. Shaking his head, Poppy was sure he was going to straighten and announce the painting was a blatant forgery.

Straightening to his full height, still shaking his head, the man turned to face everyone waiting in the small office. "There is no mistaking that signature. As Mr. Powell has already shared, the layers are there." He turned back to the painting, reversed the canvas and sighed. "And so is the patina. I have little doubt this is a Degas."

"Do you know the provenance?" Rose asked.

The man looked down and shook his head. "I don't recognize it but that doesn't necessarily mean anything."

"So we're back to finding someone to dig up the history on this baby." Adam looped his arm around his wife, who had been watching with the eagerness of a small child in a candy factory. "How good is this journalist friend of yours?"

Poppy shrugged. "I honestly don't know, but she's all we've got."

"Not necessarily." Adam pulled out his phone and snapped a quick photo.

Meg dragged her gaze away from the stunning painting. "Brooklyn?"

"Brooklyn. If there's a trail to follow someplace in the world, he'll find it."

CHAPTER THIRTEEN

"**I** can't remember the last time we played poker on the porch instead of whist." The General tossed a chip into the kitty. "It certainly makes playing with an odd number of people easier."

"You're going to have to teach us how." Meg handed over the cards for the General to replace. The woman would never be very good at the game. Her face gave it all away. The three cards were not what she'd hoped for.

"I'll take two." Dylan set down the two ill-suited cards and tried not think about the found masterpiece. He was pretty darn sure the Degas was real, but he didn't dare let himself believe it until somebody else confirmed it. He'd hoped for a flush but settled for two pairs.

From one of the rockers, Mrs. Hart put down a pad and pencil. "Anyone besides me notice Brent is still over at the Hickory cabin?"

"I did." Lucy came over with a dish of warm cookies. "Though it shouldn't be a surprise. I set them up."

Dylan had heard plenty of stories about Lucy matchmaking efforts, but with the last remark, even the General looked up at her with startled eyes. Thankfully, Lucy didn't seem to notice.

"Then you admit the refrigerator incident was on purpose?" the General asked.

This time Lucy's eyes popped open in surprise. "I think I left the oven on." She hurried off toward the kitchen.

Dylan leaned left, his shoulder brushing against Poppy's as he whispered in her direction. "What am I missing here?"

"Naomi, the gal from the refrigerator mishap, is staying in the Hickory cabin."

"Ah." He leaned back. "I see."

"This would be a first." Poppy leaned into him again. Neither seemed to be paying much attention to the game. "Not sure if that's a good or bad thing."

"Only time will tell."

Poppy's phone buzzed in her pocket. Taking a quick peek, she pushed away from the table. "I'd better take this. It's Kat. Go ahead and skip me this round."

From where he sat he could see Poppy standing on the other side of the screen door pacing and talking, but he couldn't make out any of what she was saying. Her expression was perfectly blank. Whether the report this soon was good or bad he had no idea.

Two more hands came and went before Poppy came back to her place at the table.

"Anything?" he asked.

"Not so sure. She only had time to do some quick work but was able to find information about the Millers who raised Rebecca and Deborah, nothing about her real parents in Poland. She's going to check with some folks who still specialize in connecting families from the Holocaust as well as retrieving lost art, but she doesn't have much to add for now."

"Not surprised. It's a lot of years and gaps to cover." Cards in one hand, the General scratched one of the golden retrievers with the other.

"Well, we're going home." Cindy came out of the kitchen carrying a shopping bag in one hand, a backpack over her shoulder, and the other hand a leash with the puppy pulling with all its might. "I swear, someone better fall in love with this gal soon or my shoulder's going to be permanently out of joint."

The sound of chairs scraping against the wooden porch breached the puppy's contented yaps.

"Let me help." Dylan reached for the leash and the shopping bag.

At the same time, Adam Farraday came around the table. "I was just about to say the same thing."

"Thank you," Cindy muttered releasing the hyperactive puppy to Dylan. "But I think the two of us can handle this."

"I really don't mind. My wife has me well-trained."

"Ha," Meg scoffed playfully. "Aunt Eileen had all of you trained long before I came along. Bless the woman."

"Shall we?" Dylan waved his arm toward the door and managed

to juggle the paper bag and handle.

"I can get that." Cindy failed to beat him to the handle. "I'm afraid when Lucy sends us home with leftovers, it's usually enough to feed an army. Since she knows my husband is on a deadline and unlikely to surface for air, she sent all of his favorite foods."

"No problem." The dog defied the laws of science, yanking at his arm and dancing circles around his ankles at the same time. "They say youth is wasted on the young. I think energy is wasted on puppies."

"You got that right." Cindy laughed.

He followed her around the house toward the back where she'd parked, helped load the leftovers and secure the dog in the backseat, before taking a step back. "Drive safe."

"Always." She waved and pulled out onto the driveway that meandered through the property to the other cabins.

He had just turned toward the house when a large white vehicle came to a slow stop beside him.

"How's it going?" Brent waved from the open window. "Didn't expect to see you out here."

"Just helping Cindy load up to go home. That last puppy is a handful."

"Same one from the church?"

Dylan nodded.

"Yep. Definitely a handful."

Glancing back in the direction Brent had come from, Dylan wondered if that had been the reason he hadn't come to work today. "Will we be seeing you at the church tomorrow?"

"Yeah. Had a few things to take care of today." Brent cast a glance in his rearview mirror and smiled.

"Hopefully tomorrow will be a little less crazy."

"Less crazy?"

It hadn't occurred to Dylan that Brent might not have heard the news about today's find. For a moment he considered not mentioning it, trying to keep it as much under wraps as possible, but with Brent working underfoot there was no way he wasn't going to find out about it from somebody so it might as well be from Dylan. "I gather you haven't heard about the painting?"

"I don't think so."

"Turns out that underneath the Madonna is what appears to be an original Degas."

Brent's eyes opened wide. "You're kidding?"

"Nope. Rose and an expert came up tonight to take a look at it. Poppy has a friend looking into the history."

"Wow. This could be great for the church. I know they've been hurting for money for quite some time, plus now all the restoration costs after the fire. This find could make things financially much easier on them. I'm glad for it. Some days Poppy looks like she's taking on the burdens of the church more than she should."

This wasn't the first time Dylan had noticed a glint of something he couldn't quite make out sometimes when Brent spoke to or of Poppy.

"You know," Brent continued, "she's quite a girl. I mean, all the Hart granddaughters are great, but Poppy, she's special."

And there it was. "You like her." It wasn't a question.

Brent pressed his lips together and gave him an amused smile. "Not the way you mean. But what's not to like? She's nice and sweet and friendly and concerned for my well being, the same way she is with Floyd the barber, Harry the mailman and most of the town."

"She is rather caring, isn't she?" He knew his smile was spreading but he couldn't help it.

"Glad to see it's a two way street, because if it weren't I might have to hurt you."

Dylan blinked. "What?"

"That face," Brent pointed at him with his thumb, "is the same dopey look Poppy gets when you're around her."

"She does?"

"She does. And remember what I said about hurting you. I meant it. Now I have to get going. Tomorrow's going to be a long day." Brent gave a single affirmative dip of his chin, tapped his steering wheel, pulled away and followed the driveway to the main road.

Dylan felt his grin tighten. She's dopey too. *Wow*. Could this day get any better?

• • • •

"I think this has been one of the longest days of my life." Rose kicked her shoes off and set the porch rocker in motion. "I still can't believe we're in the midst of an important art discovery."

As much as Poppy loved all the people who came and went at Hart House, her favorite times where when it was just her and a cousin or sister or her grandmother alone in the big green rockers spending time together. Now that all her sisters were married or engaged, those times were fewer and farther between. Same with her cousins. "So, what's the next step?"

"The painting will need to undergo some additional testing. Dating the paint, the wood frame, the canvas. It's always best to have a second opinion on the signature even though I trust Edward completely. And of course we need to confirm that the painting was indeed Mrs. Katz's to giveaway. Then the church can do whatever it wants with it. Sell it, donate it—"

"Put it in the church yard sale," Poppy teased.

"Wouldn't that be the deal of the century?" Rose laughed and the two fell into a fit of giggles, much they way they had when they were kids spending their summers on the lake and staying up all night playing Truth or Dare and roasting marshmallows on the beach.

"You two look pretty cozy." Grams came out with a tray of tea cups. "It's a beautiful night to relax on the porch, isn't it?"

Still chuckling, Poppy nodded. "Sure is. Where's the General?"

"He and Dylan are in your grandfather's office discussing the progress of the church renovations."

Rose leaned forward. "At this hour?"

"You have to admit, things got pretty busy around here today. What better time than the present?" Grams took a sip of her tea. "I think I'll try my hand at painting again."

"Really?" Rose glanced over her cup at her grandmother. "I didn't realize you'd tried painting before?"

"I did. Mostly watercolors."

"And some beautiful rocks." Poppy grinned up at the family matriarch.

"Well, we all know Emily and Gavin had more of a stone painting gift."

Poppy shrugged. "Beauty is in the eye of the beholder, I guess."

"Oh, good. You're still up." Adam pulled the screen door open and held it for his wife.

"We come from generations of night owls." Poppy smiled.

"I heard from Brooklyn. Is the General up?"

"Already?" Poppy asked.

"Brooklyn?" Rose muttered over her grandmother's, "He's in his office with Dylan. I'll go get them."

"Don't bother, Grams. I will." Poppy pushed to her feet and hurried inside and into her grandfather's office. "Sorry to interrupt, gentlemen, but Adam is here with Meg and says they've heard from Brooklyn."

"Already?" Dylan popped up quickly.

The General stood and two dogs in tow followed them outside.

"What have you got for us?"

"A heck of a lot more than I expected in less than twenty four hours. It seems he was able to trace the Miller family back to their hometown in Poland. From there his sources were able to determine who the Miller's neighbors had been prior to their departure that led them to the United States. It seems they were in what had once been an affluent area. One of their neighbors was a well recognized art dealer. Aaron Greenberg."

"Jewish," the General stated the fact.

"Correct. He and his wife Miriam were eventually rounded up by the Nazis and shipped to a concentration camp. Except here's the interesting part. The records show only he and his wife were sent to the camps, but records also show the Greenberg's had two daughters. Rebecca and Deborah."

"Becky and Debbie," Poppy muttered.

"Both," Adam continued, "disappeared shortly before the Greenbergs and other prominent Jews were rounded up."

A mix of emotions swirled inside of Poppy. Excitement for the discovery, sadness for Mrs. Katz' loss, eagerness to learn more, and without thought, she reached out and grabbed hold of Dylan's hand and squeezed. Delight coursed through her when he squeezed her hand back. They had come so far today. Both with the painting and with their budding relationship. And both prompted the same question—what next?

CHAPTER FOURTEEN

After all the excitement bouncing from one discovery to the other yesterday, remaining focused on the project at hand was more of a challenge for Dylan than usual. In the forty minutes or so since they had arrived at the church this morning, he'd barely managed to get tools for the day organized, and for the life of him couldn't get his mind to stop circling back around to the Degas and the family that had protected it all these years.

"Yes, Mrs. Forrester, I promise to let you know as soon as I hear anything. Yes, cross my heart." Poppy drew an X across her chest. "Yes, ma'am, really. You have a nice day too, Mrs. Forrester." The phone handle dropped into the cradle and Dylan had the feeling if Poppy could curl up in a corner and ignore the phones, she would. "How many phone calls has that been in just 30 minutes?"

He knew full well she did not want an answer to that question.

"How much longer till the day is over?" One eye closed, she glanced up at the antique pendulum wall clock and sighed again.

"Look on the bright side." He smiled at her. "The phone hasn't rung for at least forty five seconds."

"Gee. Thanks." Grabbing a nearby file, she propped it open in front of her, hand poised at the keyboard, ready to go to work, when the unmistakable sound of clacking puppy paws against the wooden floor echoed in the main sanctuary. Her head snapped up. "Uh oh."

Sure enough, the puppy who still had no name came barreling into the room and leapt onto Poppy's lap. The fact that even pulled up close to the desk there wasn't enough exposed lap for the animal to fit didn't deter the puppy one bit. Tail wagging, a paw resting upon each of Poppy's shoulders, the furball licked her chin feverishly.

"Okay. Okay. That's enough." Despite Poppy's grumblings, she couldn't stop laughing at the puppy's efforts.

"Hi." Cindy strolled in holding up a bag. "I brought her lunch. And maybe dinner."

"I gather that means we're puppysitting again today?" Poppy asked.

Cindy nodded. "You bet. I figure as word makes its way across town everybody and their godmother is going to show up here at some point today in search of the painting. What better opportunity to show this gal off and find her a good home."

"She's got you there," Dylan agreed. Just the amount of times the phone had rung since they'd arrived indicated the level of interest from the town over yesterday's discovery.

"Okay. I have patients waiting. I'm out of here. See you later." In her rush to leave, Cindy nearly collided with the pastor on his way in. A quick 'morning' and smile was exchanged and then she was out the door like a shot.

"Good morning." Pastor Bob stood at the entrance to Poppy's office. "I see we have a visitor again."

Poppy tried stroking the rambunctious pup in an effort to calm her down. "Apparently. Hopefully today we can find her a new home."

"I'm sure you will. Who can resist such a…um…interesting pup."

"Hear that?" Poppy rubbed her nose in the dog's face. "You're interesting."

The pastor took a step forward and paused. "Oh, and I'm expecting a call from the diocese attorney. When he calls, put his through no matter what I'm doing or who's in my office."

"Will do." Poppy continued to stroke the dog. "Bad news?"

"I sure hope not. The bishops would like to confirm what we are indeed the sole owners of whatever this painting turns out to be."

"Understood." As soon as the pastor was securely planted in his own office, Poppy turned to Dylan. "I sure hope Mrs. Katz's father wasn't trying to smuggle illegally obtained paintings from the country."

"I'm sure if he had underhanded motivation, he would have given each girl a painting to smuggle, not just one between them."

"I suppose you're right." The puppy seemed to be settling down on her lap. "So, where are we going to keep her today?"

"Right where she is looks pretty good from here."

"Well, it might look good to you, but how am I supposed to get any work done?"

"That is not what you asked me, what you said was *where shall we keep her* and I pointed out that she looks quite content right where she is. You didn't say a word to me about whether or not you could work while she's here."

"Everyone's a critic," she teased.

He was actually mildly surprised to see the puppy curled up on her lap. Dylan hoped the dog wasn't going to grow too big or whoever adopted her was going to be pretty surprised to wind up with a full-sized lapdog.

"Poppy," the pastor called from the other room. "Can you put your hands on the original donation file for Mrs. Katz?"

"Sure." She shifted the puppy from her lap to the comfy chair across from her desk. "Now you be a good girl, I'll be right back."

Dylan resisted the urge to shake his head. He wasn't convinced that puppies had it in them to obey instructions. He wasn't completely convinced adult dogs had it in them to obey instructions either. But at least this time for whatever reason, the little gal appeared happy to remain curled up in the seat.

"Yoo hoo."

In the short time he'd been working with the church he'd come to recognize the diversity of callers. That particular *yoo hoo* sounded an awful lot like Louise Franklin. If he had his names and faces and voices correct, this would be the woman from the local pharmacy who had access to just about every person in town. If she heard, there was no chance in the world they would be able to keep incoming news of the painting under wraps.

"Yoo hoo."

"In here," Dylan called.

"There you are."

He must've been in town longer than he thought because he had guessed correctly. "How are you doing today, Mrs. Franklin?"

"Now, you know you should be calling me Louise. We've been through this before."

"Yes, ma'am." For whatever reason he wasn't terribly comfortable calling her by her first name. Maybe it was because of her age, or the respect his military family had drummed into him, or the tendency for the name Thelma to be associated with Mrs. Franklin's Louise in almost every conversation.

"Well, I suppose that's better than Mrs. Franklin. Is the pastor in?"

"I believe he's on a conference call."

"Then it's true?"

Talk about an open-ended question. By now she had to know it was absolutely true but he'd go ahead and play along with her. "I'm sorry, what are you referring to?"

"Why the painting, of course."

"Of course. The painting. Well yes, we did find a painting hidden under another canvas. And we do believe it could be a very valuable painting, but we won't know for sure until Rose takes it back to Boston for some more scrutiny."

"I see." The older woman tapped her foot rhythmically, or perhaps impatiently. "Do we know how long that will be?"

He felt like saying we don't know anything, but settled for a simple, "I'm afraid not."

"Very well. Please tell Poppy and the pastor to let me know as soon as there's word on the situation."

"Yes, ma'am." There were a lot of people who wanted to be first to know. He did not want to be in the pastor's shoes on this one.

"Was that Louise Franklin?" Poppy walked into the room as the woman reached the front doors, marched through, and didn't bother to pull them closed behind her.

"It was, and you're welcome."

"For what?" Her nose crinkled in the cute way it did when she was confused, then she waved her hand. "Never mind. Louise Franklin. Yes. Thank you. One less person for me to have to repeat the story to and probably at least a hundred more I won't have to because she will." Poppy circled the desk and came to a fast stop. "Where's the puppy?"

"In that..." Dylan pointed at an empty chair with his small brush. "Chair."

Poppy pulled her desk chair back and looked underneath, then spun around looking at each corner of the room, then twirled back around. Her mouth dropped open, her eyes circled wide, and her head snapped in the direction that Louise Franklin had just gone. "The front doors were open."

"Oh, crud." Dylan dropped his brushes on his work table, grabbed a nearby towel and trotted toward the door after Poppy.

The woman he'd come to realize he was falling in love with—okay, was in love with—stood at the top of the church steps, a pinky hanging in each corner of her mouth, and whistled louder than he had ever heard from a human mouth. They each looked left and right, hoping the puppy would appear.

Poppy's eyes widened with concern. "Maybe we should have given it a name after all."

"We'll find her." A car whizzed past them on the main drag, and for the first time since he'd arrived, Main Street suddenly looked like an especially busy thoroughfare. He didn't say anything to Poppy, but his gaze darted further up and down the street, thankful not to see a furry bundle lying in the road.

She whistled again, followed by a, "Come here, girl. Come on. I have a biscuit for you."

Willing to admit it or not, Poppy had become quite attached to that energized furball. Apparently it didn't take long for woman or puppy to work their way into someone's heart. He tried whistling and calling for the dog, but nothing. Puppy had to be somewhere, somewhere safe he hoped, hopefully not halfway to Boston, because already he didn't like the sadness in her eyes. He just had to find this dog.

● ● ● ●

How was she ever going to explain to Cindy that she lost the puppy? And how was she ever to live with herself if they didn't find her? "Come on, girl," she called again. "Come on." Nothing.

All her whistling and calling had brought the pastor out on his office, and now he was walking up and down the neighboring properties, calling for the puppy that had no name. Two of the church's neighbors had noticed her efforts and now they were whistling and calling in their own side yards and alleys. Still no sign of her.

Poppy had walked halfway around the church and back again, and was now walking around the other way. Dylan had done the same thing in the opposite direction and now they were coming together in the middle of the church side parking lot. "I don't understand where she could have gone."

"She has to be somewhere." But where, he wondered. Where would a curious puppy go? "Puppy, where are you?" A muffled woof, or what sounded like a woof, caught his ear. "Did you hear that?"

"Maybe. Or maybe it's just wishful thinking."

He walked closer to the building and called again. Another muffled sound filtered through. "There. Did you hear that?"

"Yes. I think I did," she said with a bit more enthusiasm, walking right up to the old stone church. "Come on, girl. Bark louder."

Another sound came at them, even louder than the one before. "It's coming from the back of the building." He trotted to the end of the church and called again. This time the responding bark was crisp and clear. Dylan looked around. "There." He pointed to a lone open basement window on the back of the building.

"How the heck did she get in the basement?" Relief washed over her. At least they'd found her. "Come on," she called over her shoulder, almost running back to the church. At the front steps, she called over to one of the neighbors, now searching their front walkway again. "We found her!"

The way she ran into the building and down the hall, anyone would have thought they were out to rescue a young child and not a four-legged puppy. In her eyes, both were just as helpless, though if she had to admit it, a puppy was much better qualified to go up and down a flight of stairs than a toddler.

"I wonder who left that open?" Dylan pulled the basement door all the way open, flipped the light switch on, and followed her down the stairs.

"Well, look at that." Poppy came to a stop at the foot of the stairs. Straight ahead of her, curled into the corner, her head on a small pillow, the dog looked as content as a babe in its mother's arms.

Laughing at the sight before them, Dylan shook his head. "Looks like she's a thief too. Isn't that cushion from your office?"

Poppy let out a sigh. "It is. Come on, girl. Let's go back upstairs now."

The dog didn't move. Front paws crossed, she looked up at them through big brown eyes.

"I don't think she wants to." Dylan smiled and walked up to her. "Come on, girl."

The dog responded by putting her head down on her paws.

"Okay, Missy. Enough is enough." Poppy walked right up to her and just as she was about to squat, the pup sat up, exposing what had been trapped under her paws.

"Oh, my." Her hand slowly reached out, her fingers timidly touching the top of the small piece.

Poppy's moves were so guarded, her attention so focused, even though he wanted to wrap his arms around her, he didn't dare touch her for fear he'd startle her. "What is it?"

"A pendant." Her voice was barely audible. "One my father gave me."

"Oh." He still wasn't sure if he should hold her, touch her, or if she needed space.

Fluffy, Missy, or whatever her name would be, solved his problem for him. The dog had no qualms about what Poppy needed: a good strong lick on her cheek.

An unexpected chuckle broke the silence and clutching the pendant in one hand, Poppy scratched the dog with the other. "Thank you. I have no idea how you found it, but thank you."

"Has it been missing long?"

She nodded. "About three or four years ago. Daddy bought it for me at the state fair the year before he died. I wore it all the time. Then a few years ago I was working at my desk, reached for it and realized the chain had broken and it was gone. I was heartbroken. I have no idea where it fell, but somehow this gal found it. It's times like this that make me wonder if maybe dogs aren't just one of God's angels."

When she extended her hand to him, he accepted the piece. Time, or the basement, or wherever it had been hiding, had not treated it well. An alabaster stone of sorts, something was painted on it. A flower. He had to look at it a long time to conclude it had probably at one time been a poppy, her namesake.

As she hugged the furry pup, a smile graced her lips. It seemed this old church was full of surprises. He couldn't help but wonder if it held any more secrets.

CHAPTER FIFTEEN

"Lucy has graciously agreed to share her breakfast recipes." Meg Farraday stabbed at her French toast casserole. "This is just to die for."

"It's one of our favorites too," Grams said with a smile. "It was originally my grandmother's recipe. Generations before us had such a different attitude on waste. Nothing was discarded, everything found a purpose, even stale bread."

"Well, I for one am delighted your grandmother came up with the recipe. Best stale bread ever!"

"I'll have to make the chocolate depression cake later," Lucy said with a smile. "Lots of good recipes came from our grandmothers and hard times."

"Sorry I'm late." Dylan came in and pausing to flash a quick smile that felt like it was meant for only Poppy, made his way to the buffet.

"Fresh hot sausage here." Large plate in hand, Lucy crossed the room. "Oh heavens, you guys must really be hungry. We rarely go through two whole breakfast casseroles."

"I'm afraid that's my fault." Meg wiped the corner of her lips with her napkin and waved two fingers at the housekeeper. "I can't seem to resist."

A smile as wide as the lake took over Lucy's face. "Then I'd best bring out the last one. I'd intended to wrap up individual slices to donate to the church yard sale tomorrow, but I can bake another later when I bake that depression cake." The woman who had been taking care of the Hart family for as long as Poppy could remember, practically skipped out of the room. Nothing seemed to make Lucy as happy as finding someone new to feed.

"Do we have any updates this morning?" Dylan carried his plate back to the table and set his dish down next to Poppy, flashing another only for her smile.

"Nothing more from Brooklyn." Adam shook his head.

The General looked to Poppy. "And from Rose?"

"Painting should be delivered sometime today." That same night after arriving at the lake, Rose arranged for insured and temperature-controlled transport of the painting for first thing the next morning. Considering it had been hanging on a wall in an old stone church for years, Poppy thought that the temperature-controlled thing might be overkill, but if it made everyone happy what did her opinion matter. Experts were on hand in Boston ready to pounce, and in little more than twenty-four hours, the painting's authenticity had been confirmed. The church was officially the proud owner of a missing Degas. The decision had been made to return the painting to the church until it could be decided what to do with it. Of course, due to its size and how well it was concealed in his office, the General's safe was the storage unit of choice, though Poppy wasn't sure where the temperature-controlled thing came into play.

A text message sounded on her phone. Pulling it out of her pocket, she glanced down and quickly read a note from Kat. "Oh, boy."

"From Rose?" Grams asked.

Poppy shook her head, her gaze instinctively going to Dylan first, whether for support, for answers, or something else, she had no idea, but she found the way his hand swiftly made its way under the table to grab hold of her free hand an instant comfort. "It seems Kat wants us to read her piece in the *Times*."

"*New York Times*?" Meg asked.

"She didn't say, but if it's a Kat piece, the AP is probably picking it up and it will be everywhere."

"Be right back." The General pushed to his feet and while Poppy sorted through her phone, her grandfather returned to the table, his tablet in hand. "We've been outed."

Quickly he read aloud the article describing the discovery with a lot more flair than a simple *he removed a canvas to find another underneath*. The town of Lawford was prominently displayed, the name of the church, even Dylan's name as the person accredited for both the discovery and the restoration of the church murals. In the end, every Tom, Dick and Harry would know about the painting and where to find it. Not exactly what the church diocese had in mind.

"So now what?" Grams asked.

The General set the tablet on the table. "We'd better let Pastor Bob know. If we thought tomorrow's yard sale was going to be busy, now it's going to be downright bursting at the seams with people."

Another text notification came in, this time on Adam's phone. "It's Brooklyn. He wants me to call. Any objections if I put him on speaker here at the table?"

All heads moved from side to side. Everyone was eager to hear what the man had to say.

"Hey, how's it hanging?" Brooklyn announced loudly to the table.

Grams, being the epitome of an old-fashioned lady, hid her smile and focused on her meal, pretending not to have heard the casual and colorful greeting.

"I'm at the breakfast table with everyone. We're anxious to hear what you have to say."

"Oh, excuse me. Of course. As you probably know by now, Degas was rather prolific and he had a handful of recognized paintings missing since the Nazi era. A few have recently been discovered in Paris where a descendant of a Nazi art dealer has been hoarding them. None of those seem to fit the description of what you've found."

Adam ran his hand across the back of his neck. "I sense a *but* coming."

"You do. From what we've been able to dig up from the available records of reported stolen artwork, there is a woman in upstate New York. Jocelyn Hodges. She's eighty-seven years old, sharp as a tack and has been looking for not one but two Degas that were taken from their home the night her father was dragged off by the Nazis."

"Jocelyn sounds French."

"Her mother Marie was French and her father Frederick was Dutch and a prominent art collector who fought for the resistance."

"He wasn't Jewish?" Poppy asked.

"No, the Kleins were not, but he was one of the many who saw what was going on and refused to stand by and watch. More than just the Jewish population were sent to the concentration camps. Frederick Klein died at Auschwitz."

A heaviness settled over the room. Forks stilled. The meal was over.

"Anyhow," Brooklyn continued, "one of my people spoke with her and as you can imagine, after all these years she's very excited at the possibility that this might finally be one of the two."

"I see." Adam's tone reflected what everyone in the room thought. If the original painting was indeed taken by the Nazis, then the masterpiece wasn't Becky Katz's to donate.

• • • •

So far the news wasn't what Poppy wanted to hear. For the church's sake, she'd hoped the painting was theirs to do as they pleased. So much good could come from the money it would bring. And the remainder of the restorations wouldn't have to wait. Her gaze drifted to Dylan. She still wasn't completely sure if given the chance whether or not he would stay on to do more work, but she sure as heck hoped so.

"There's more," Brooklyn's tone lowered and Poppy braced herself. "Has anyone seen the morning paper?"

"Yes. We have," Adam said.

Brooklyn continued, "Kathleen Regatta works fast. The thing is, it's going to be very hard to discreetly uncover anything else now that the news is out."

"That's what I was thinking," the General muttered.

"Since it gave away your location, I hope you're prepared for the impending onslaught."

"That bad?" Poppy asked.

"Whenever a painting of unknown origin appears, people come out of the woodwork with stories of their long lost family heirloom. No matter how deep in the mountains you live."

Poppy knew this wasn't going to be easy, but she hadn't considered just how complicated it could get. What was Kat thinking going public so fast?

"Just be careful, some of these folks are pros at playing the victim. They and their stories can be quite believable."

"We will."

"In the meantime," Brooklyn continued, "we'll keep digging. Also, the church should expect a call from Margaret Bask. She's Becky Miller's granddaughter."

"You found her?"

"We found her mother, Becky's daughter. The granddaughter found us."

"I don't like the sound of that."

"Too soon to tell. She asked a lot of questions. Apparently, her grandmother died when she was a little girl and her mother cut off all ties with the aunt. Debbie's daughter married into a church that believed they were the few saved and the rest of the world was going to hell. Especially the Jewish aunt."

"Oh, dear." Grams' eyes circled round. "Well, I suppose at least we'll all be in good company."

The people in the room laughed freely and Poppy resisted the urge to go hug her grandmother to pieces.

"That may be the nicest thing anyone has ever said to me." Brooklyn seemed half sincere and half teasing.

"Anytime, Mr. Brooklyn." Grams was grinning at the phone on the table.

"Brooklyn, ma'am. Just Brooklyn. Anyhow, we're gathering as much background on the Bask family as we can to present to the church, but if they connect the dots of our inquiries and the newly found painting… Well, let's say your upstate New Yorker may not be the only person laying claim to the artwork."

The board of directors were still in debate over the legal and ethical ramifications. What would Mrs. Katz have done had she known their father's treasure was a priceless Degas? The consensus was that it would not have been given to the church, but a few members insisted a gift was a gift. According to their attorney, the law saw it the same way.

"Hate to break up this party." Lucy came in with a large empty tray and began gathering the buffet dishes. "But Thelma and Louise are here to start loading for the sale tomorrow. We've got work to do."

Chairs pushed back and people picked up their empty plates. With the regular folks out in search of a bargain, and the masterpiece looky-loos about to descend on Lawford any minute, the church really was going to have their hands full. Maybe things wouldn't turn out so bad. Out the window she spotted the cars already lined up, ready to load the goodies they'd collected and take them to the church for set up. Yeah, the chances of it not being so bad tomorrow were as good as her shot at marrying a crown prince.

● ● ● ●

"What are you up to?"

The feel of Poppy's fingertips on his shoulder had startled him. As much because he was focused on the stretching as he was by the gentlest of touches that had sent shooting through his system all the way to his toes. "I had a few minutes between steps and thought I'd go ahead and re-stretch the Madonna."

"Do you really think Mrs. Katz's father painted this or was it just a story?"

"Well, if her father's middle initial is M, then it makes sense. When you stretch it to the proper fit, you can see his initials in the far bottom corner. AMG."

"I wish she were still here to see this."

Twisting about, he craned his neck just far enough to place a soft kiss on her temple. "I never met her, but I wish I could have."

"Everyone liked her. She was a petite thing, but a fireball."

"Reminds me of someone I know." He couldn't resist and placed another gentle kiss on the same spot as a moment before. "Poppy?"

"Mm." She'd leaned against him now and didn't seem inclined to move.

"Have you given anymore thought to how the pendant got into the basement?"

"You know," she pushed back and tipped her chin up to see him, "I have. I rarely go into the basement. I think in five years I can count the times on one hand that I ventured down there for something so I know I didn't drop it down there. But staring at the radiator yesterday, I noticed the gaps between the planks in the floor."

His gaze followed the direction she was pointing in. Without words, the two immediately gravitated closer to the old heater.

"In the winter this thing is always too hot or too cold. It's not unusual for me to play with the valve at the base. Actually, struggling with would be more accurate."

He wasn't following where this was going, but knew she'd get to a point soon.

"Look over here." She leaned over the antiquated radiator, her hair dangling between it and the wall. "See there?"

Following the direction of her finger, at the base of the radiator, between the ironworks and the wall, the gap from the floorboard to the baseboard was indeed wide enough for something like a pendant, if angled just right, to slip through. "I'll be."

"I really think that's how it wound up down there."

"Makes as much sense as the dog finding it somewhere else and taking it downstairs."

"Well, we don't have puppies here very often—not at all actually." She chuckled and stepped back. "I think God just wanted me to have it back and the puppy was the only one curious enough to do God's legwork."

Dylan nodded, and smiled. "There are some people who think dogs are God's angels on earth."

"Well, I'm not so sure if that would be true for Missy, but maybe."

"So, she's going to officially be Missy?"

"We can't keep calling her girl and who knows how much longer it will be till Cindy finds her a home."

"Maybe today at the beauty shop will be the day."

"Maybe."

For some reason that response didn't sound as upbeat as it should.

"So where is the pendant?"

"At home."

"Not going to wear it?"

Her fingertips brushed against her collarbone and now he understood why he'd seen her do that from time to time over the last couple of weeks. A habit that didn't die with the lost pendant. "Maybe sometimes but not every day. Not anymore. Besides, it's pretty sloppy looking. I need to get it to a jeweler to fix the attachment piece and at least clean it up, but someone who won't make it worse. I don't want to lose all of the poppy."

"Well, as it happens, I know a lot of good jewelers who can be trusted to restore fine jewelry."

"It's just a state fair craft piece."

"There's no such thing as just a craft piece. It's a beautiful piece of art that matches a beautiful lady I know."

Like before, she leaned against him a bit more heavily than a few moments ago and rested her cheek against his shoulder. "It's going to be really hard going back to working here without you someday."

With a mind of their own, his fingers lifted up and brushed back a lock of dark hair. He was just thinking the same thing too. Very hard.

CHAPTER SIXTEEN

"We might as well put a revolving door on the church." Frustration showed on Pastor Bob's face. Yesterday had been insane. Today was unlikely to be any better. Not only were the townsfolk popping in unannounced to see the Madonna that had been on display and virtually ignored for years, they all expected to find the Degas just hanging out in the open in the sanctuary. Neither he nor Poppy had gotten much done work-wise. "I sure hope the board makes up their minds soon. We're simply not equipped to be responsible for a masterpiece worth millions."

"Millions," she repeated softly.

Suddenly she wondered if stashing the painting at her grandfather's was the best idea the old man had ever had. It wasn't like they had some sophisticated security system.

Yes, the gun safe in his office closet was immoveable, but its design was for a different purpose. And while it might be true that burglars don't like houses with dogs, Lady and Sarge simply were not trained to keep burglars away. All in all, maybe they should re-think the plan.

"Everyone in town is ready. The tent flaps should be opening in less than five minutes." Louise Franklin stood at the doorway. "The crowds should be spilling over this way soon. Already we have some people milling about here instead of lining up for the tent sale."

At almost the last minute, everyone on the sale committee agreed the donations were too much for the church parking lot so instead they went with keeping the sale out at the Point and surrounding grounds at Hart House. The tent was the best idea they'd had yet.

When Poppy had left this morning, the line of shoppers waiting already wrapped around the tent and up to the main road. At least with the tent, everyone could prep inside and man their posts before the troops stormed, and safely close up the leftovers for tomorrow. Two days of sales. She suspected two very long days coming.

"This painting may be the best thing to happen to the sale." Thelma Carson came hurrying up the steps and stopped next to her Merry Widow friend. "We've got a good size line outside. Can I start the tours now or do I have to wait five more minutes for the official opening time?"

"Tour?" She and the pastor echoed the same solitary word in the same flustered tone. Poppy was pretty sure she was blinking madly.

"Yes. People want to see the original painting, where it was found, etc. The board approved the idea. It's only a dollar a person. I'm the guide till noon then Nadine takes over this afternoon. Nadine and I will split the shift tomorrow after services. Besides, now that the sale is over at Hart Land and not on Main Street, the church where the discovery was made will attract shoppers back to bolster the local sales."

Pastor Bob threw his arms up in the air. "See. Revolving door. No need to tell me what's going on. I only work here." Sucking in a deep breath, the pastor blew it out slowly, forced a casual smile and opened his mouth. "Thank you, Thelma. I'll just lock up the offices. If anyone needs me, I'll be working on my sermon from home." Still trying hard to maintain a calm smile, he turned to Poppy and Dylan. "You guys can either help with the sale or take the day off. Whichever you prefer. You've both worked hard the last couple of weeks. A day off is well deserved."

"The lines were pretty long at Hart Land this morning. I think I'll go see if I can help," Poppy said softly.

Dylan repeated the same. Neither of them had been at the church long enough this morning to start on their day's work, so he extended his elbow and smiled. "Shall we?"

Poppy's only assignment had been to help collect donations. She hadn't even been part of the set up for today, but she was willing to roll up her sleeves if asked.

"Oh." Cindy stopped short half way up the stairs when she spotted Poppy and Dylan leaving the building. "I was going to leave this girl with you."

As soon as the puppy spotted Poppy, her tail began swishing back and forth and her rump started swaying like a flag in the breeze. Danged if Missy wasn't the cutest ugly puppy she'd ever seen.

"I'll help," Dylan offered. "If you need me, that is."

Oh yeah, she needed him, more than she should. "Thank you."

• • • •

So far, the morning with the puppy had gone without mishap. Every so often Dylan would take the dog for a stroll away from the people for her to do her business and then come back. Except this time he didn't see Poppy, and wasn't able to track her down amid the growing crowd. Though he had noticed her favorite spot seemed to be the baked goods table, even though her figure belied her sweet tooth.

Just as he got within hearing distance of the table, shaking her head, Lucy shoved her hands onto her hips and turned to Fiona Hart. "What the hell has gotten into Harriet?"

Both brows climbed high on Mrs. Hart's forehead. "Excuse me?"

"That woman is smiling so wide I think her face might crack."

"Smiling?" Fiona Hart turned to scan the immediate area, most likely for the Harriet woman.

"You heard me."

"Is that unusual?" Dylan wasn't sure why he asked, the women's reactions made it pretty clear smiling was not Harriet's thing.

"That woman hasn't cracked a smile since she graduated kindergarten."

"Now, Lucy. She isn't that bad."

This time Lucy raised both her brows and dipped her chin staring upward at her employer.

"Okay, so maybe she tends to frown a bit."

Crossing her arms, Lucy continued glaring.

"All right. I don't know. It's a lovely day. This is all for a good cause. Maybe she decided to join the human race." Both Fiona Hart's hands slapped over her mouth as her gaze darted left and right. "I didn't say that."

Dylan shrugged. "I didn't hear a thing."

"Thank you." Mrs. Hart smiled.

"By any chance, have you seen Poppy?"

Both ladies shook their heads.

"I think this is one of her favorite tables."

"Hers and a lot of other people," Fiona announced as proudly as if she'd baked all the donated goods herself. "Sales seem to be quite strong. We've had to restock a few times and pretty much all the tables look less crowded than a few hours ago."

"Everything is selling like hot cakes," Lucy added. "Guess there's a reason the expression one man's trash is another man's treasure has been around for so long."

"You mean because it's true?" Mrs. Hart flashed her signature demure but knowing smile.

Dylan chuckled. "That would be one reason."

"Oh Fiona, I've been looking for you." A short blonde woman, a little on the heavy side, came right up to Fiona Hart and hugged her tight enough to crack a rib. "I am so sorry about your marbles."

"My marbles." For anyone listening, it would be hard to know if that was a question or statement, but Fiona Hart didn't let on for a moment if she was confused by the declaration.

"I let Kathy Martin take the blame."

This time Fiona's perfectly arched brows came together in a V. "Kathy Martin."

"No one ever liked her anyway. I just wanted you to know I'm so sorry. Really I am." And with that, the woman gave Fiona Hart one more bone crushing squeeze and practically skipped away whistling an unfamiliar tune.

"What was that all about?" Lucy asked.

"Well," Fiona turned, still frowning, "Kathy Martin moved away at the end of second grade. But I'm pretty sure she is apologizing for taking my bag of marbles."

"Excuse me?" Lucy glared at her boss once again.

Fiona bobbed her head. "I had a beautiful collection of marbles. I was very proud of them. Then one day they disappeared. In first grade. Never saw them again."

"That's crazier than Harriet smiling like a loon." Lucy shook her head.

"What is getting into people?" Callie walked up to the table with another tray of donated goods from Lily's Pastry Stop. "Jerry from the garage just asked Edna on a date."

"He what?" Lucy and Fiona echoed.

Callie transferred the lemon heather donut holes onto the near empty dishes. "You heard me. Jerry walked up to Edna's table, bowed at the waist, then grinning like the Cheshire Cat asked her to join him for dinner after the sale. And," she held one finger up from each hand, "get this—not just any dinner invite. To the Cattleman's Steak House in Boston. Only the best for the best, he said."

"Jerry said that?" Lucy somehow managed to ask without closing her open mouth.

Callie bobbed her head.

"Did someone spike the punch?" Dylan was kidding but the way the three women's heads snapped around in his direction and then all looked to each other and tipped their heads, they must have seriously considered it.

Finally, the family matriarch dipped her chin in confirmation. "I'd better go check."

"And fast," Lucy added, "before we get a confession to something truly criminal or all the old geezers in town get down on one knee and then can't get back up!"

Dylan held back a laugh. It all had to be a coincidence.

"There you are." Poppy trotted up to him, quickly leaning down and cooing at the dog while rubbing behind both her ears.

He felt oddly jealous of the mutt.

"I can't believe how many people are here." Poppy pushed to her feet, the dog wiggling at her side. "The General has planted himself on the porch with a dog at each side."

"Really?" Fiona Hart asked.

"A lot of people are here just to see the painting the papers talked of. They seem to think it's just hanging on our walls since it's not at the church."

"Why in heaven's name would they think that?"

"I'm not sure. I actually read the article a second time to see if she said it was being kept in our safe."

"Oh, my," Mrs. Hart said. "Kat would never do that. Though she did mention your grandfather was supervising the situation."

"I suppose that might be all some people need to put two and two together and come up with Hart House." Poppy let out a deep sigh. "I just don't understand why Kat thought putting this out in the public eye would help us track down the painting's history. I mean, I know she said that this was the fastest way to get solid leads, but she neglected to mention it's also the best way to be overwhelmed by the curious."

"And the liars," Lucy added. "I heard Cora on the restoration committee saying that since that article hit the news yesterday, they've received no fewer than one hundred and five claims of ownership."

"Good grief." Poppy covered her mouth with one hand.

The number was startling to Dylan as well. He knew there would be disreputable people trying to make a fast buck, but he underestimated how many. Lifting his gaze in the direction of the house, he wondered seriously for the first time since all this came about if perhaps the idea of professional art thieves to contend with might not be very real. "I think I'm going to check on the General."

"I'll come with you."

His first instinct was to say no, he'd handle it himself, but his second thought shoved that aside. The odds of any real danger were slim to none and the prospect of having Poppy at his side was always welcome. Very welcome.

Halfway up to the house, an older woman flanked with two men about her parents' age slowed her steps as Poppy and Dylan approached. "Excuse me."

"Yes," Poppy spoke first.

"I was told at the church that the pastor is unavailable and I should come here to speak to Poppy Nelson. Would you happen to know her?"

"Very well." Poppy smiled. "I'm Poppy."

"Oh. Excellent. I'm Jocelyn Hodges and I've come for the painting."

CHAPTER SEVENTEEN

"**Y**ou'd better call the pastor," Dylan whispered to her.

Random thoughts and a sense of sheer panic scrambled around inside her, much the same way Missy danced around her feet. Sucking in a long deep breath, she nodded at Dylan and did her best to think clearly. "We should go to the house." Poppy gestured at the large white house that stood like a monument to life and family for the Harts.

"Thank you." The woman smiled softly and glanced ahead.

"It's a long walk, Mom." One man extended his elbow.

"Nonsense." The woman batted at the offered arm and almost growled at the other gentleman when he opened his mouth to speak. Both stepped aside and let the older woman take the lead.

Poppy really didn't want to like this woman, but so far the lady had managed to put her completely at ease, and make her smile. This meant another dilemma reared its head. If she liked this lady who had a claim to the donated painting, who was she going to root for?

Years of military training and marriage to her grandmother prevented her grandfather from being anything short of hospitable to a visitor. Especially one of respectful age, even if the place felt overrun by the curious. Already on his feet, he glanced briefly at Poppy, no doubt making a rapid assessment, and nodded politely to the approaching woman. "Good afternoon."

"Good afternoon," the woman repeated. "I've come for the painting. I'm Jocelyn Hodges."

"I see." The General stepped to one side, allowing her passage onto the porch and into the house. He did not, however, feel the need to extend the same courtesy to the two gentlemen at her side and immediately followed her, leading the group to his office. Directing Mrs. Hodges to take a seat across from his desk, he circled the old piece of furniture. "I do hope you won't take offense, but we would like to see some identification please."

"Of course." Her son standing at her back, Mrs. Hodge reached into a compact handbag and removed her wallet, then her identification, and extended it across the desk.

The General carefully examined the document, lifted his gaze to the woman, and then once again studied her New York driver's license. "Why don't you tell us about the painting, Mrs. Hodges."

"I don't know how much of the story you have been told. My father dabbled in art collection. Before the war we were doing well. My father was a respected physician in the long line of bankers. I was eight years old the night our front door burst open and what felt like an army of Germans hauled my father out of bed, and out of the house. I remember my mother running after them, crying and pleading that it was all a horrible mistake. When my siblings and I followed after her, she huddled us into her arms and sat us down on the living room sofa, doing her best to reassure us through her sobs. I remember my youngest sister asking where they were taking Daddy. All Mother could say was not to worry. Several more officers stomped through the house, every room. All our valuables had been sold or hidden, except for two Degas paintings in my sisters and my room.

"We loved them so, considered ourselves ballerinas. We danced around the room and made up all kinds of fun stories, twirling about in full skirts. Thinking back on it, I suppose my father didn't want to disappoint us by taking them down. Under the circumstances a rather foolish choice, but it helps me understand how much he did love us. More than the price of a valuable piece of art."

Okay. Now Poppy really liked this woman. The church could find another way to raise needed money.

"I can speak as a father and a warrior that your father no doubt loved you even more than you think."

Poppy batted her eyes quickly. She never had had any reason to doubt her grandfather's love for his daughters or granddaughters, and yet that statement made her understand how much deeper his feelings ran than she could understand. She'd almost lost the battle with pooling tears when Dylan's hand inched onto her lap and folded her hand in his. Amazing how one person—the right person—could make such a difference in her world.

"If you please." Jocelyn straightened her spine. "I would like to see the painting now."

"Of course." The General scanned the people in the room, glanced out the windows, and proceeded to the closet door. Inside he pulled on a hinged mirror and exposed a massive vault. His back to the room, he maneuvered the combination, opened the door, and turned to face everyone, a long tube in his hand.

Every eye in the room was riveted to the General's every movement. Closing the vault and the closet, he approached Jocelyn and took the empty seat beside her. "Is this one of the works stolen from you?"

Slowly, fingers almost trembling, the old woman accepted the canvas scroll and gently almost caressed the rolled artwork open. The moment the painting was fully exposed, a tired smile graced her lips. "I remember this well."

Poppy's heart sank for the church but rejoiced for the end of this woman's long journey.

"It used to hang over the sofa."

Sofa?

"My father worked with the resistance. At times they needed more money than they had. My mother explained to me that many works in his collection were sold to raise funds. He especially liked working with a Polish art dealer who worked with an underground railroad of sorts to help Jewish children escape Nazi controlled territories."

Jocelyn's words had Poppy nearly holding her breath.

"This painting was sold a year or so before my father was taken. My father called him Mordechai, but my mother called him Aaron. I don't think I ever knew his last name." The woman sat back, slowly rolled the painting up once again and blowing out a low sigh, held it steady. "It's almost funny for one so young, there are some things that are deeply imbedded in my memory, and yet, I can not for the life of me remember my neighbor's name, or what my favorite food was."

"I'm not at all surprised." The General nodded. "I still remember the first day I saw my future wife and have no idea what I did the rest of that day."

The words brought a smile to Jocelyn's face. "I suppose my search shall continue, but I thank you for bringing a few moments joy at the sight of this lovely piece."

"Thank you," Poppy blurted, "for sharing that story with me. I knew Mr. Greenberg's daughter."

"Greenberg?"

"Aaron M. Greenberg. I suspect the M is for Mordechai. It fits with the woman I knew and the stories she told that her father would have been as caring as your father."

"I'm glad."

As if wanting to add her agreement, Missy gave a loud bark and lunged onto her hind legs, tugging hard on her leash.

"Down, girl." Dylan pulled her back. "I'm sorr—" The rest of the words fell flat as the dog lunged again, capturing the roll from Mrs. Hodges and bolted through the open door before a hair-raising scream ripped from the old woman's throat.

"No," Poppy screeched and darted over a hassock and after the dog. This could not be happening.

• • • •

"Are you sure you don't need to sit down, Agnes? You've been here for hours now." Fiona had known Agnes Cartwright since school, and in her old age, thanks to that sweet tooth Agnes had developed diabetes and then a whopping case of neuropathy. Fiona couldn't believe the woman had not only signed up to help, but had been on her feet without a single complaint.

"Nope. I'm fine. Doc has me on some new supplements that have been doing wonders."

"Oh, I'm so glad to hear that." Whenever she could, Fiona tried to use one of her grandmother's home remedies rather than prescription meds but she wished she'd had the wherewithal to have asked for more before she'd lost her grandma.

A customer loaded with bags of goodies leaned over the table, scanning the baked goods. "Any more of those Nutella brownies?"

"You're in luck. Last one." Lucy plopped the wrapped treat onto a plate and handed it over, collected the two dollars and turned to Agnes. "Your daughter's brownies are a hit."

"I keep telling Millie she should sell them at the Creamery, but she says they're just for us. And of course, fundraisers like this. I have one for dessert every night."

"Every night?" Fiona didn't like the sound of that with a diabetic, but then again, if her new treatment was working, who was she to interfere.

"Yes. She gets in a baking mood and then we freeze a bunch. The batch she made for the sale today looked a bit dried out to me so I went ahead and unfroze some and brought those instead."

"Seeing how much everyone likes them, I'm glad you did."

A tapping sound reverberated over the loudspeaker and then a very sour rendition of la la las echoed through the tent.

Fiona tipped her face upward at the unsettling sound. "What *is* that?"

"Let me entertain you!" blasted suddenly over the loudspeaker.

"Who the heck?" Lucy stood up on a nearby folding chair. "Good grief. You won't believe it."

"Believe what?" Fiona stretched her neck in an effort to see the back of the tent where the PA system was set up.

"It's Grace McGowan."

"What?" This Fiona had to see. She marched down to the next table and stood on the chair. Sure enough, quiet, introverted, retired librarian Grace McGowan was not only singing the famous song—off key—from the musical *Gypsy*, the woman was doing leg kicks and twirling a scarf.

"Did you check the punch?" Lucy called from her perch.

"Yes." Maybe she should have checked again.

"Good heavens, what is going on here?" Millie, Agnes' daughter, came up to the table. "I was just coming to see if you're ready to go home. Who the heck is that?"

"Grace McGowan," Fiona muttered, climbing down from the chair. "I think I'd better go save her from herself."

"Too bad we're out of the brownies. She really enjoyed those. Must have downed at least three or four of them." Lucy climbed down from her spot as well.

"Oh, yes." Agnes turned gleefully to her daughter. "Your brownies were a hit."

The young girl looked momentarily confused. "You mean the

ones we donated?"

"Oh no. Those looked all dried out. I unfroze some of the ones you bake for me and brought them instead. Good thing I brought an extra bag."

In an instant, Millie's jaw dropped and her eyes circled wide as saucers, then her head whipped around in the direction Grace's crackling voice came from. "Oh, Mother."

"Stop!" a loud female voice called from the opposite end.

Millie froze in place. "Oh, hell."

This time a male voice coming closer shouted, "Grab her!"

"Oh, Mother." Millie sighed. "Now you've done it."

"Out of the way," still another voice yelled, just as people started separating like Moses and the Red Sea.

"I've always wanted to see the inside of the jail," Millie muttered.

Lucy drew her attention away from the shuffling crowd and growing murmurs coming their way to look at Millie. "What?"

"Those are Mom's medical brownies for her neuropathy." Millie sighed hard and shook her head.

"My what?" Agnes' head spun around.

"For the love of God, someone grab that dog!"

As the shoppers backed out of the way, Fiona could see a fluffy and fast puppy with a leash dangling from his neck and a roll of paper sticking out of its mouth, galloping down the aisle. "That's Missy."

"And Poppy and Dylan behind it." Lucy waved a finger at Millie. "Grab that dog!"

Ralph at the next table lunged for the dog and tripped over Louise. The dog sprinted over the fallen bodies. A few people registering the calls for help reached out but the dog ducked under a table and now had another puppy yapping at her heels and in on the chase as well.

"Watch out for the painting!" Poppy called.

"Painting?" Fiona mumbled. "Oh, no."

CHAPTER EIGHTEEN

Painting clenched tightly between her teeth, the wayward puppy ran all the way to the shore, picking up four legged comrades along the way and a crowd of two footed onlookers. At the water's edge the puppy dropped the trophy painting in exchange for a plastic beach shovel someone had left behind.

"It's pretty damaged." Poppy stood in the sand holding the crumpled and slightly soggy canvas, opening it to display multiple teeth marks. She looked on the verge of tears.

"Here," Dylan took it from her hands, "I happen to know a pretty talented restorer."

Poppy's face brightened slightly as she reached down to stroke the cause of all this trouble. "You really did do a very naughty thing."

"Only you would say something sweet to the dog after all this." Dylan surveyed the unrolled canvas and frowned.

"That's what I would have explained if you and Poppy hadn't bolted out of the office so quickly." The General stood at the edge of the lawn, gesturing at the damaged artwork.

"This is a print," Dylan confirmed.

The General nodded. "The original is still at the museum with Rose. They have the equipment to make rapid reproductions for marketing purposes. We felt it was best in light of all the publicity if people believed we had the painting."

"That was awfully risky, don't you think?" The puppy had managed to wiggle its way into Poppy's arms. "I mean, what if real burglars had shown up?"

The General waved his arms. "We had a plan."

"You always have a plan, don't you?" Dylan asked, even though he knew the answer.

"Anyone want to update me on what the heck is going on?" The sheriff joined the crowd that had gathered at the edge of the property. "Our switchboard blew up. Stolen art, pack of wild dogs, illegal drugs. What the heck have you people been up to?"

Poppy walked up to the sheriff and held out the puppy. "This would be the wild dog."

The sheriff laughed and scratched under the little gal's chin. "Not surprised. And the art. Did someone come after the painting?"

"That would be this guy." One of Jocelyn's sons stood by a man in handcuffs and flashed a badge attached to his belt. "Spotted him climbing in the window while the rest of the world was chasing the dog. He was in the safe tossing the contents when I went back in."

The sheriff handed the dog back to Poppy and took the man in cuffs off the son's hands. "Do I want to know what the illegal drugs part of all this is?"

Poppy and the General wore matching expressions of confusion. Others shook their heads and shrugged. Only Dylan seemed to notice the unusual silence and tight lips coming from Lucy and Fiona.

"Well, then. I'd better get this guy processed." The sheriff nudged the perp forward.

"I'd be interested to hear who this character is. My money is on an idiot who saw an opportunity and ran with it, but you never know." Jocelyn's son shrugged. "I'll be by later to get my cuffs back."

"Sure thing," the sheriff called over his shoulder.

Scratching the dog behind its ears, Poppy looked to her grandmother and Lucy, who had fallen in step beside her. "I wonder where the drugs phone calls came from."

"Maybe from the same person who reported the pack of wild dogs," Fiona suggested.

Lucy picked up her pace. "There's another hour left to this show. I'd better get back to my post and make sure someone's taken the mic away from Grace."

"You may want to give her some black coffee too," Fiona suggested.

"Black coffee?" Poppy asked. "What for?"

"Goes good with brownies," her grandmother said, catching up to her husband.

Yep, if there was one thing Dylan had learned in his time here, it was that Fiona Hart was as wise as she looked and probably twice as smart.

• • • •

"What a perfect night for my favorite dinner." Poppy's grandfather reached for another slice of soda bread. "And it's always all the nicer when good friends can join us."

Even though Dylan, and Adam and his wife were guests at the table, the comment was most likely meant for Katie, who joined them for dinner.

"Doesn't hurt that this guest came bearing your favorite bread." Katie smiled at the General. It was clear she was as fond of the Hart family as they were of her.

"I can't believe what a whirlwind week this has been." Adam shook his head and stabbed at his corned beef. "Life is going to seem pretty boring when we head home tomorrow."

"Well, we're certainly glad you could join us," Grams offered.

"I do hope you can make it our way some day so we can return the hospitality." Meg smiled at the older woman. "I've learned a lot this week about family inns. Thank you."

"Our pleasure." Fiona smiled. "And I hope to see you again soon. Either here or in Texas."

Poppy looked at Dylan beside her. He seemed awfully quiet. Her gaze shifted to her family gathered at the massive dining room table. All her sisters were there with their significant others and a few of her cousins too. Mostly nowadays she only saw all of them at the same time when someone got married. Zinnia's wedding was next on the list and then they'd all be wed. In a few more years the place would be hopping with Hart great-grandchildren. Wouldn't that be a blast?

"I understand Mrs. Katz' niece contacted the pastor directly," Lily said to the group.

"That's right. Kat is doing a follow up article on the painting's authenticity and the story of the Mrs. Katz's escape from the Nazis. Turns out, with a little help from Brooklyn she got a lot more information on the work Mr. Greenberg and other prominent Jews did during the Hitler years and is going to add that to the story. She reached out to the niece for her perspective and the niece called the pastor."

"And?" Callie asked.

"The painting is probably worth millions," Poppy stated the obvious. "And the niece agreed that without the church, the painting might never have been discovered, so everyone seems to agree that an amicable and fair resolution would be to split the proceeds in half. The church will get a much needed full restoration and be able to supply many of its pet charities, and Debbie's remaining family will get the other half."

"Seems very civil," Alan, Cindy's husband, said. "As a writer, my mind had already gone in a completely different direction, playing out all the nastiest and goriest of possibilities. Right down to family skeletons in the closet and gruesome murders to keep the money all to one person."

"I suppose you're never going to write a romantic comedy?" Cindy laughed.

Alan kissed his wife sweetly on the lips. "'Fraid not."

"I think fate is a wonderful thing." Katie held up her wine glass. "To all the blessings on Lawford Mountain."

"Here, here," a choir of voices repeated.

"Which brings me to this dog." Cindy cast a glance in the direction of the kitchen where the puppy was happily curled up in a massive crate that Lucy had stuffed with some of Grams' failed quilt projects and a huge leftover ham bone, and then stared pointedly at her sister. "She's the only one who no one else seems to want. You're the only one who thinks she's sweet."

"She is. When she's not creating havoc."

"And you're the only one who scratches her ears when she's done creating havoc," Cindy pointed out with a wide smile. "That dog, my dear sister, is meant to be yours."

"Oh, no." Poppy waved both hand in front of her frantically. "The pastor would kill me if I brought Missy to work every day and she can't stay home alone."

"See!" Cindy shouted. "You've named her. I'm telling you, that dog is yours. You two are meant to be together."

"Desserts are leftover baked goods. Too many to cart in here. They're all on the island tonight. Except for Millie's brownies." At Lucy's heels, the dog marched behind her. "And this one is tired of being cooped up. So, everyone to the kitchen."

Chairs skidded back on the wooden floors. Dishes and silverware clanked as folks picked up their empty plates. Callie muttered, *what was that about Millie's brownies* and the dog came right up between Poppy and Dylan and looking first at Poppy, softly set her head on Dylan's lap, glancing up with big brown puppy eyes.

"Seems that dog is yours too," Katie spoke softly, patting him on the shoulder as she walked past, leaving them the last two in the room.

"Maybe you could take her home with you to Texas. When you go, I mean." Those words had been harder to spit out than Poppy had imagined.

"About that." Dylan sucked in a deep breath and pulled a small velvet bag from his pocket. "Your mom got this for me."

"Mom?" Poppy watched him empty the bag onto his palm. "My pendant."

He nodded. "I thought maybe if it were restored…"

In the palm of his hand, he held out a beautifully cleaned stone with a lovely red flower. A poppy. "Did you do that?"

He nodded again.

"It's beautiful." More beautiful than she remembered.

"You don't mind?"

She shook her head. "I love it even more. Thank you."

Sucking in a long heavy breath, he blew it out fast and removed a thick gold chain from the bag. "The new clasp on the pendant won't break. You can wear it anywhere you like."

His hand extended, she placed the pendant in his palm again and waited while he strung it, then nudged the puppy aside and stood to clasp it around her neck. "There you go."

"Thank you." She squeezed the restored piece in her hand. She would treasure it forever.

"And now. About the dog."

Lifting her gaze, she saw that he had moved beside her and the dog. "I think Cindy's right, you two belong together."

"You do?" the words barely eked out.

"And I think Katie is right too."

She didn't understand.

He blinked a long moment and leveled his gaze with hers. "I

think we all belong together. I think," he swallowed hard, "I think I'd like to move here, give life in Lawford a chance, give us a chance. And when the time is right, I'd like you to consider making us a real family."

"A family?"

Lips pressed tightly together, he nodded. "I already know I love you, Poppy Nelson. If it wasn't that normal people don't propose so fast, I'd ask you to marry me here and now."

"You would?" Her voice actually squeaked.

"I would. What do you think?"

"I think I'm not going to need near as much time as you think."

His eyes rounded and the corners of his mouth shakily tipped upward until a bright smile took over. "I think I like that idea."

"Good. Turns out, I love you too, Mr. Powell, and Missy here needs a real home."

From the hall, the General had his phone at his ear and peered around the doorway just long enough to see his last single granddaughter slip into the arms of her perfect match.

"You there, Harold?"

"I am." He straightened. "Told you we got it right."

CHAPTER NINETEEN ~ EPILOGUE

"G uess this is still the place to be." Jake smiled at the crowd already gathered around the biggest fire he'd seen since his teenage years. Back then everyone in town knew everyone, and hanging out on the Point or the beach at Hart House had been the place to be. The difference tonight, perched at the head of the massive circle of family, the General and his bride of decades, Fiona Lawford Hart, sat comfortably in two Adirondack chairs.

Leaning forward, Cindy's husband Alan sat behind her, gently rubbing her shoulders as she quietly poked at the fire. Lily let go of her husband Cole's hand to reach into a cooler. "Name your poison." she said to Jake.

"Whatever beer you have. Thanks."

"You," Lily addressed Heather, "I don't have to ask. Always on call. One caffeine free pop coming up."

Taking a seat between her two sisters, never pulling free of her husband's careful hold of her hand, Heather nodded, rolling her eyes.

"Don't let them tease you." Nestled against Dylan, her soon to be husband, Poppy, the only cousin dressed in a long flowy skirt, let go of his hand and waved a finger at her cousin Heather. "Saving lives is important."

Having Heather living on the mountain now, and saving lives as Poppy put it, a stone's throw away instead of in big city Boston, had only added to the familiar childhood dynamic tonight.

Callie undid her hair, stuck a big toothy clip between her teeth, twirled the golden ponytail into a sloppy bun, then clipped it all back in place atop her head. Retaking her husband's hand, she quietly leaned back against him, displaying the sheer peace and contentment that came with a starry summer night, family, and oodles of love.

Still sporting that glowing grin that came with all new brides, Zinnia didn't bother releasing her new husband's hand and instead raised them both to wiggle her fingers in greeting at her arriving cousin and her husband.

"Nothing in this world beats the tranquility of the lake." Violet smiled at her husband beside her. The man, who had been watching his wife the way some might admire a clear evening sky or blooming flower, lifted the hand he held and gently kissed her wrist. Her eyes sparkling into his, she whispered softly, "Well, almost nothing."

Digging her toes in the sand, Rose held onto her husband's arms wrapped around her waist and let herself enjoy the moment. "Looks like all we're missing now are Iris and Eric."

A car door slammed shut, followed by two shadows strolling hand in hand down the path toward the beach.

"Oh good. I'm ready to start the s'mores." Poppy grinned at no one in particular.

"You're not going to find any of those in Italy," Heather teased.

"Of course not. She can't even take advantage of the handsome Italian hunks." Violet shifted in the sand and squeezing his hand, winked at her husband.

"True. Italy is the home of the David statue." Iris shrugged.

Lily sighed. "Oh for heaven's sake. Who wants s'mores when you're going to have three glorious weeks of real Italian food?"

Poppy giggled. She was looking forward to having Dylan show her *his* Italy. The churches, the museums, and most of all, the Sistine Chapel.

"Lily does have a point." Dylan smiled at his soon-to-be wife. They'd talked about everything under the sun to do with Italy, and Ireland and all the places she'd dreamed of going, but for their honeymoon they'd settled on the place that had meant the most to both of them. "But man does not live by bread alone."

Cackles, and giggles, and groans, floated around the fire at the corny use of the standard biblical line.

"Why don't we do this more often?" Lily shifted to grab another pop.

Cindy gathered the skewers Lucy had brought outside earlier. "Probably because the only time all nine of us are here is when one of us is getting married."

"Don't say that." Poppy frowned. "After our wedding this

weekend there won't be anyone left."

"Hm." Violet straightened. "I hadn't thought of that."

Grams shook her head. "And you shouldn't think that way. The circle of life continues. When your mothers one by one married and then moved away, I thought the end of our little world was immanent. Then each of you was born and joy merely took on a new perspective and eventually we were all together again."

"Who has the marshmallows?" Poppy inched forward, surprisingly content with the simple analogy.

"Me." Callie grabbed a bag beside her. "Graham crackers are here too but I don't see the chocolate."

Zinnia waved her fingers, passed the bag around and shrugged. "You know I like chocolate."

The cousins and their mates all chuckled. Grams and the General hadn't stopped smiling.

"So what we need is a good game of Truth or Dare." Callie popped a marshmallow on a skewer.

"Oh, good grief." Heather rolled her eyes. "We're not ten anymore."

"Okay," Callie nodded. "Just truth. How's the gig at the new hospital working out?"

"Actually," Heather smiled, "really well. It's nice doing the same work without the bustle of the big city."

"Good. Who's next?" Callie dangled her skewer over the blazing fire.

"I have a truth for the General." Cindy held her marshmallow over the fire without looking up. "Was it really allergies all those months ago?"

The General's smile slipped.

"Tell them, dear. It's time." Fiona Hart's arm stretched out and covered her husband's hand.

"Yes and no."

"Oh, well that's clear as mud." Violet's attempt at humor fell a bit flat.

"I did have allergy trouble and the dizzy spells were from fluid in my inner ear, but Heather was right in that some of the changes in my life were more serious." Several gasps were heard and he held up his hand. "I said *were*. Just over two years ago I was diagnosed with bladder cancer."

Heather's jaw dropped. "You didn't tell me."

"I didn't tell any of you, or your mothers. I had outpatient surgery to clean it all out and went on once a month immunotherapy treatments—"

Cindy cut him off. "The monthly specialty shop visits that stopped."

It wasn't a question, but the General nodded just the same. "I have had a clean bill of health and expect a long, cancer free life ahead of me."

All heads turned to Heather. Her gaze darted about a moment and then she nodded. "I'll make sure, but what he's saying does make sense. Some cancer treatments have come an amazingly long way with excellent results and prognosis. But," she waved a finger at her grandfather, "you and I will talk later."

"Yes, ma'am."

"I have one for the General." Heather quickly dropped her heated marshmallow onto a graham cracker. "Was the broken shower handle coincidence?"

Jake tipped his head. "I wouldn't mind hearing the answer to that. I always thought it odd that after all these years, that was the night I was invited over to play cards."

The General crossed his arms, leaned back, and studied the current generation of Hart family members, then nodded. "Okay. Since we're laying our cards on the table, I might have tinkered with the handle before Heather got into the shower."

"I thought so." Jake bit into his gooey s'more.

"Wait." Lily leaned forward. "You planned that?"

"I had help," their grandfather admitted.

"Who?" at least half a dozen voices sounded off.

The General chuckled, and Jake bobbed his head. "My grandfather."

"Him too," Harold Hart admitted.

"Too?" Lily asked.

Alan pushed his glasses up the bridge of his nose. "Surely you've noticed that our grandfathers all just happen to know each other?"

"That is rather a large coincidence." Lily nodded.

"No coincidence about it. We were talking about how long so many of our grandchildren were taking to get married. Then we started discussing personalities and interests and we figured out that Heather and Jake were meant to be. That's when I realized if I wanted great-grandchildren I was going to have to give you all a nudge."

"Surely you had nothing to do with Lily hitting me?"

The General chuckled. "No, not even I am that good. Lily mowed you down all on her own."

"I did not." Lily's spine unsnapped as all her family glanced her way. "I mean, I did tap him a little, but I didn't mow him down. He ran into me."

"You stick to that story, sweetheart." Cole kissed his wife on the cheek. "Besides, you were definitely worth it."

"What I don't understand," Dylan spoke up, "is how no one noticed the West Point connection."

"Who said we didn't notice?" Zane blew on a chocolate dripping s'more. "We just didn't catch on."

"Well, I can promise you all that I am officially retired from the matchmaking business." He glanced at his wife and smiled.

"Only because you're out of granddaughters," Callie muttered.

"Not true. That is, of course I'm out of granddaughters, but you must admit I'm nine for nine."

"You mean unlike Lucy, who has been at this for years and is still striking out?" Violet teased.

"Not so fast." Lily leaned forward. "Brent and Naomi seem very happy together. I think there's a wedding in their future."

"Maybe," Rose shrugged, "but there's no way of knowing if Lucy was actually responsible for that."

All heads turned and focused on Rose.

Eyes opened wide in response, Rose's shoulders deflated and she sighed. "Okay, maybe two people locked in a walk-in refrigerator per Lucy's direction does have her matchmaking fingerprint all over it."

Heather blew her sister a kiss. "I thought you were smarter than that."

"So tell me one thing." Poppy twisted to face her grandfather.

"Did you set the church on fire on purpose?"

"Absolutely not." There was no wavering, no hint of cover up in his tone.

"Good." She relaxed again.

"Sometimes," he looked to Lily, "Fate is more creative than I am."

"That's not possible, dear." Fiona Hart patted her husband's hand. "But nice of you to give her credit anyhow."

"Speaking of truths." Iris turned to her grandmother. "That oil painting of the Point is out of this world fantastic."

Grams grinned broadly. "Thank you. Dylan is a wonderful teacher."

Dylan shook his head. "I can't take the credit for your talent."

"If you'd seen my watercolors, you wouldn't say that."

The crowd laughed, more skewers were held over the fire, more stories were shared, followed by more laughter, and lots of love. Always love.

● ● ● ●

"Doesn't she just glow in her mama's wedding gown?" Fiona Hart had spent most of this day beaming almost as much as the bride.

Like his wife, Harold Hart had been watching his youngest grandchild carefully. The sparkle of sheer joy in her eyes was enough to keep him smiling for the rest of his days.

"Did we look that much in love on our wedding day?" Cindy reached for her husband's hand, but the question hadn't been directed at anyone in particular.

"Of course you did," Fiona Hart replied without removing her gaze from the couple cutting the cake. "Still do."

Alan Peterson grinned at the older woman's words and kissed his wife on the temple. The whispered *I love you* was intended only for his wife, but Harold had excellent hearing. The words lifted his heart as much as they did Cindy's.

"Oh look. She's making him wait till she's done chewing." Fiona clapped her hands and chuckled. "That girl does love her cake."

"Fortunately for her, that man does love that girl." Lily blinked back tears of joy. "Someone want to tell me when she grew up?"

"What are you talking about?" Cindy swiped quickly at her cheeks. "You're almost as young as she is."

"Ooh." Fiona's hand shot out, shushing her granddaughter's chatter. "I say she shoves it all over his face."

"Grams!" Cindy chuckled. "How many of those mimosas have you had?"

"Don't be silly." Fiona waved off her eldest Nelson grandchild. "It's just always a little more memorable when there's a little more of a mess."

Everyone watched as Poppy's fork lifted up into the air and with careful aim, she advanced tipping the medium sized piece directly in his mouth. No muss, no fuss. A bull's-eye.

"Oh, well." Grams smiled. "It was still fun to watch."

"Ah. Look." Callie almost spit out the sip of tea she'd just taken. Poppy had snuck another bite of the delicious cake and while Dylan looked to the coordinator for instruction, his bride plopped a dollop of icing smack on the tip of his nose.

"Here, let me help," she murmured and every camera within view went off as she kissed his lips, got a smidgeon of icing on her own nose, and kissed the remaining icing away from Dylan. A second of long held gazes, a wide smile, a silent conversation no doubt referring to settling this later, and Dylan kissed away whatever was left on her face.

"The perfect match, those two." Pride resounded in the General's voice.

"Absolutely," Fiona agreed.

The hum that precedes a microphone announcement from the DJ sounded. "All married couples please join the bride and groom on the dancefloor."

One thing Harold Hart never let pass him by was a chance to dance with his wife. For so many decades the opportunities were few and far between. For too many years he was away more days than he was home.

The floor was packed. People of all ages glided along to a variety of wedding standards played from Elvis Presley's *Can't Help Falling in Love* to Ed Sheeran's *Perfect*. Bit by bit, the DJ requested that couples married only one year retake their seats. Then those married five, then ten, and on down the line until the only two couples left on the floor were the newlyweds and General and Mrs. Harold Hart.

Poppy's mother stood in front of the DJ, a mic in one hand and a glass of champagne in the other. "To my precious daughter and new son, watch and follow the example that has been set and you will forever be as happy as you are this very moment."

The sound of clinking glasses echoed softly throughout the room.

To seal the deal, Dylan leaned over and gave his wife a sweet but firm kiss on the lips.

Nine girls happily married. Callie had a point the other night. Though she got there in a roundabout way. What was a retired Marine general supposed to do with his time now that he was out of single granddaughters?

From Lily's Recipe Box

CHOCOLATE DEPRESSION CAKE
(or Wonder Chocolate Cake)

What you'll need:

1 ½ cups of flour
½ tsp salt
1 tsp baking soda
3 tbs cocoa
1 cup of sugar
6 tbsp oil
1 tbsp white vinegar
1 cup water

Instructions:

Pour all dry ingredients into an 8x8 or 9x9 inch ungreased baking pan
Stir together dry ingredients with a fork
Make 3 holes in the ingredients with a spoon or your finger
Add the following:
  In 1st Hole: 6 TBSP oil
  In 2nd Hole: 1 TBSP vinegar
  In 3rd Hole: 1 tsp vanilla
Wait a short while (maybe fifteen or thirty seconds)
Pour 1 Cup of Water evenly over all & stir with a fork until well blended
Bake at 350 for 30 minutes
Cool then frost in the same pan... remove the 1st slice with a spatula… quite moist and yummy!

Lily's note: *This is a versatile favorite because it's VEGAN!*

MEET CHRIS

USA TODAY Bestselling Author of more than a dozen contemporary novels, including the award-winning *Champagne Sisterhood*, Chris Keniston lives in suburban Dallas with her husband, two human children, and two canine children. Though she loves her puppies equally, she admits being especially attached to her German Shepherd rescue. After all, even dogs deserve a happily ever after.

More on Chris and her books can be found at
www.chriskeniston.com

Follow Chris on Facebook at ChrisKenistonAuthor
or on Twitter @ckenistonauthor

Questions? Comments?
I would love to hear from you.
You can reach me at chris@chriskeniston.com

www.ingramcontent.com/pod-product-compliance
Lightning Source LLC
Chambersburg PA
CBHW031417200726
48285CB00017BA/2423